DOUBLE DECEPTION

Elizabeth Law

Walker and Company
New York

First published in the United States of America in 1987 by the Walker Publishing Company, Inc.

Published simultaneously in Canada by John Wiley & Sons Canada, Limited, Rexdale, Ontario.

Library of Congress Cataloging-in-Publication Data

Law, Elizabeth.
  Double deception.

  I. Title.
PS3562.A857D6   1987   813'.54   86-28219
ISBN 0-8027-0950-8

Printed in the United States of America

10 9 8 7 6 5 4 3 2 1

Prologue

"MISS TURNBULL WISHES you to attend in her parlour, if it is convenient."

The maidservant, having given the conventional summons, dipped a courtsey and waited.

"I wonder if she's discovered that I've been reading the poems of Lord Byron," Anne thought. His works were strictly forbidden to the young ladies of the Turnbull Academy but, during an afternoon's chaperoned expedition into Plymouth, she had contrived to elude Memoiselle's Roché's watchful eye and slip into a bookshop. The volume itself was wrapped in a plain cover, and she had taken care to read it only in the privacy of her cubicle, but it was generally asserted that Miss Turnbull had eyes in the back of her head.

"I'll come at once," she said now, dismissing the maid with a smiling nod.

Even if she'd been found out, there was not very much the principal could do about it. At eighteen, Anne was due to leave school anyway, so there would be no point in expelling her. It was possible that her guardian would be informed, but Lord Sinclair had so far been distinguished by the complete lack of interest he'd displayed in his dead brother's only child. Of course there had been the family quarrel, which had resulted in her own father's marrying a young lady, regarded as unsuitable and, after her death in child-bed, burying himself on his Devonshire estate while his brother had gone north and proceeded to increase the Sinclair fortune in Yorkshire.

Anne, recalling that she had said "at once," smoothed down her dress, checked that her hair was neat, and made her way down the staircase and across the hall to the small chamber known privately to the students as the "bullring," but used by Miss Turnbull as a sanctum whence she could keep her finger on the pulse of her establishment.

The lady herself was seated behind the flat-topped desk on which, as usual, were ranged the green blotter, the onyx jar containing a number of sharpened quills, the deep inkwell. There was a bright fire crackling in the grate, the leaping flames vying with the thin spring sunshine beyond the windows, reflected in the silver coffee service laid on a gate-legged table between two wing chairs. A glass-fronted cabinet held a variety of small china ornaments, and on the walls several embroidered samplers reminded the onlooker that "Home is Best," "A Stitch in Time Saves Nine," and "Patience is a Virtue."

Miss Turnbull was said to be in her midforties, a rumour she herself had initiated, neatly lobbing ten years off her age when she had opened the Academy fourteen years before. With an eye to the future, she had deemed it wiser to be younger rather than older when she advertised for pupils. Sarah Turnbull had in fact been born in seventeen-sixty; she had been educated by a father who believed in the value of higher education for girls and a mother whose selfish individualism had made her only daughter into a refuge from all the tasks and problems of the real world. Sarah had fetched and carried, run the household, studied Latin and Greek with her father, and, after a typhus epidemic had carried both of them off within the space of three weeks, found herself in her fortieth year with a large house and a small income. She had mourned for a year for the parents to whose faults she had always been blind and taken a further year to plan her curriculum, to engage staff, and to find pupils.

After fourteen years, the school, though she preferred the term "academy," was flourishing in a quiet way. There were never more than twenty pupils, girls from excellent backgrounds, though to absolve her social conscience she occasionally took a poorer student. Her small staff was loyal and competent, and she herself knew every detail of every part of the running of the place. Though she had been a plain, sallow girl, in middle age she had acquired a certain distinction, her grey hair upswept in a style sufficiently outmoded to reassure anxious parents, her bosom upholstered beneath stays that creaked slightly when she moved.

When the polite rap came on the door, she laid down the letter she had been reading and called "Enter" in her clear, carefully modulated tones.

The girl who entered was dressed in the modest manner considered de rigeur for Turnbull students. Her high waisted dress of blue voile had a lace fichu tucked in at the neckline and cuffs of matching lace on long tight sleeves with tiny shoulder puffs. From the wide blue sash that was looped gracefully below the small bust, the skirt fell straight to a ruffled hem. It was a garment that was extremely flattering to a slender figure, and Anne's figure was both slim and supple. It was a pity that her face lacked the fashionable flower-like delicacy which sent Romantic poets into raptures. Anne Sinclair was not plain, but her chin was slightly too square, her eyes more grey than blue, her fair hair apt to droop no matter how assiduously the curling tongs were applied. She had been blessed with a clear complexion and white even teeth, and her hands were exquisite, but her gaze was too direct and the set of her mouth too unyielding to please any connoisseur of female beauty. It was fortunate that she was exceedingly wealthy and would be able to make a good match; unfortunate that she would probbly find it politic to conceal her intelligence from her bridegroom.

"You wished to see me, ma'am?" Anne's voice, rich and deep, was one of her greatest attractions.

"Indeed I do, Miss Sinclair. Won't you sit down?"

Evidently the volume of Lord Byron's poems had not been discovered. One was not invited to sit for a scolding. Anne took the nearer of the two wing-backed chairs, folded her hands in her lap, and waited.

"I have received a letter from your uncle, Lord Buckfast Sinclair, who is, of course, your guardian." Miss Turnbull picked up the letter again and tapped it with a well-cared-for nail.

"Yes, ma'am?" Anne looked politely attentive, but her interest was caught. Letters from her uncle were rare. She couldn't recall more than a handful in the eight years she had been at the Academy. "He writes to say that now that you are eighteen it is time for you to 'come out' in society. However, as the London season proper does not begin until the autumn, he considers it best that you travel up to his Yorkshire estate and spend the summer there. According to his letter, social amusements are not entirely lacking in the North. You may peruse the letter for yourself."

Miss Turnbull, coming from behind the desk, handed Anne the crested notepaper and, taking the other wing-backed chair, began to pour the coffee.

4

The arrogant masculine hand was starkly black against the silky paper.

Sinclair House,
York.
3rd May, 1816.

Dear Madam,

As my niece and ward, Anne Sinclair, is now eighteen, her further schooling is at an end. As the London season does not commence until the autumn, I have determined that it will be more convenient for her to spend the intervening months here where there will be gaieties in the form of private suppers and informal balls, which will afford her the opportunity of meeting young people of her own age. Lady Tatlock, who is a neighbour, has kindly volunteered to act as duenna and to supervise the purchase of whatever is necessary for my niece's emergence into society. I enclose details of the transport available and look forward to a speedy reply,

Your obedient servant,
Buckfast Sinclair.

"He does not sound very much like any kind of a servant, obedient or otherwise," Anne said, her lips quirking slightly as she returned the letter.

"Lord Sinclair writes very civilly," Miss Turnbull reproved. "He has spent most of his life in Yorkshire, has he not? Doubtless he has picked up a certain bluntness of manner and speech."

"The word I would choose is 'uncouth.' "

"But not, I trust, a word you would use." Miss Turnbull looked faintly shocked. "Since your father's death he has been responsible for your well-being and he is discharging his duty."

"With no great enthusiasm." Anne made a small face though her coffee was sweet. "Why, ma'am, since my father died and he brought me here, my uncle has not troubled to visit me once. He has not even visited Lucy House, though its upkeep and administration is in his hands. No! he entrusted everything to the estate manager and the solicitors, and the house itself was immediately rented out to strangers so that I could not even go to stay there during the holidays."

"We did try to render your periods of leisure attractive." The principal looked slightly offended. "Also you had the companionship of those young ladies whose fathers, being stationed in outlying corners of the globe, could not enjoy the company of their children when term was ended."

"Yorkshire is not an outlying part of the globe," Anne flashed, and bit her lip. "I beg your pardon, ma'am. You must not fancy I am criticising you or grumbling at the fact that this has been my home for the last eight years. I have been very happy here, and I am most grateful for the education I have received, but you must allow me a little impatience when my uncle, having dropped me here like a parcel, expects me at the snap of his fingers to uproot myself and travel into Yorkshire."

The other, who privately agreed, passed a small dish of wafer biscuits and took another sip of her coffee before saying, "You do not remember your uncle?"

"Only very vaguely. Papa had just been killed by the fall from his horse, and there were people coming and going. It is all somewhat blurred. I recall his wrapping a greatcoat around me and my falling asleep in the carriage—it is all confused."

"The mind has a way of shielding us against remembered pain," Miss Turnbull murmured. "Doubtless you were very shocked by your papa's sudden death—you do not remember him either?"

"Again, it's like fragments recalled from a dream," Anne said slowly. "He was always singing and very sociable. There were always friends coming to Lucy House but again—" Her smooth brow puckered. "I can recall times when he was not there, and I was with the servants. You never met papa, of course."

"Only your uncle. He had just become Lord Sinclair by virtue of your father's death, and I spoke with him for only a few minutes." She remembered the tall, dark man who had seemed to be holding not grief, but anger in check; the fair-haired child with the dazed unhappiness in her eyes and the resolute expression of someone determined not to cry.

"The whole matter was arranged very swiftly as you know," she continued. "When your uncle came he brought the documents proving his guardianship and reimbursed me for a year in advance. He judged it better for you to remain here rather than pay regular visits to your old home, lest such interruptions prove upsetting. I have felt bound to comply with his wishes—you were not thinking of returning there to live? With the house rented and—well, you are certainly too young to set up your own establishment."

Anne shook her head and put down her coffee cup. "No ma'am. I don't come into control of the estate until I am twenty-one anyway. My uncle did mention that in one of his letters," she said. "I don't believe that I would enjoy seeing strangers occupying it. But I don't particularly wish for a season either, whether in

London or York. To be honest, it strikes me as a great waste of time and money to educate a girl and then expect her to simper behind a fan until she has caught a husband."

"My dear Miss Sinclair, I do trust that you have not derived such notions from anything that you may have learned here," Miss Turnbull said in alarm. "I do admit that we try to achieve a higher standard of scholastic ability than in most academies of learning for young ladies, but I would be greatly distressed if it had implanted in you any unfeminine ideas. Education fits a girl for matrimony and at the same time, should poverty or single blessedness be her lot, enables her to earn her living."

"And I am rich," Anne said simply, her lips quirking again. "Pray do not scold me for being so vulgar as to speak of it, but I am well acquainted with the terms of my father's Will. Now that I am eighteen, I am permitted to draw upon the interest accruing from the capital—"

"Subject to Lord Sinclair's approval."

"And when I am twenty-one, or married—whichever comes first—I come into control of the whole, save that if I am married it will be my husband who controls it. My course in life is already charted."

"A course many would envy." Miss Turnbull envied it a little herself.

"As you say, ma'am." The lips were firm, the voice level.

"Do you wish to write to Lord Sinclair yourself?" The other was rising, the signal that the interview was at an end.

"The missive was addressed to yourself, ma'am. I would be grateful if you would reply, informing my uncle that I am ready to comply with his wishes," Anne said, also rising.

"I am informed that Yorkshire is a delightful county—very bracing," Miss Turnbull said.

Anne, dropping a curtsey, merely smiled slightly. Inside she was seething, but her natural reticence precluded any open display of temper. In any case the blame could not be laid at the principal's door. According to her lights she had performed her function admirably—too admirably, Anne thought, opening the side door that gave onto the garden. Finding in Anne an intelligent mind, she had been at some pains to train it, without pausing to consider that such a method might have unforseen consequences.

To go to Yorkshire and embark on the tedious round of social events designed to display a wealthy young lady to her prospective suitors was the last thing Anne wanted to do. The trouble was that there was no way in which it could be avoided. Her uncle was also her guardian, and she was dependent upon his approval even if she wished to use the interest on her inheritance. She kicked a stray pebble on the path and scowled at it. One summer was all she craved; one summer during which she could be free to discover what she wanted out of life, free to explore the feelings that bubbled beneath her quiet surface, feelings that were stirred by the books she read.

She had even begun to write herself, snatching odd half hours to jot down her impressions of the other students, the teachers, the occasional visitor who came. She hid the sheets at the back of her sketching folder and wished she knew someone who could give her an unbiased opinion. She had sufficient material for a short book. Its theme had already stirred in her mind—an account of one year in the life of a maiden lady who earned her own living by teaching school. She even had a title, *Season of A Spinster*. All she required were the three months to write it.

Once she was in Yorkshire under the chaperonage of Lady—what was her name?—Tatlock—she would be caught up in a whirl of dress fittings, shopping expeditions, visits to stupid people who would push their unattractive sons forward as prospective bridegrooms. Anne, who had read sufficient about the fashionable life to despise it, scowled more ominously than before and turned off the main path towards a gazebo placed among the shrubbery. In the fourteen years since the Turnbull Academy for Young Ladies had been opened, the gazebo, with its pillars and fretted trellis, had become a spot where the girls went when they wished to think over something quietly by themselves.

Today the little building was already occupied. A girl with light brown hair held by a ribbon that matched her dark dress sat on one of the wrought-iron benches, one hand idly shredding the leaves of a vine that twined up the trellis. Her face was pensive and, as Anne approached, she heaved a sigh loud enough to be heard.

"You sound sad today, Anna." Anne stepped inside and sat down on the bench next to the other.

"Oh, pay no attention. I am in one of my melancholy moods." Anna Sayle shook her head as if she were forbidding herself to feel such a childish emotion.

"I am in a bad humour myself," Anne said. "My uncle, who has almost ignored by existence for the last eight years, has written demanding my presence in Yorkshire, where I am to be launched upon the social scene. I shall have to go to balls and supper parties and dress up every single day—why are you smiling?"

"Oh, to hear your grumbling about a fate that most young ladies would rush eagerly to embrace strikes me as ironic," Anna said. "My own fate is not so pleasant."

"Are you still determined to accept the post in France?" Anne gave the other an anxious look.

"I cannot remain here any longer on what is virtually charity." Anna made a restless movement with her hands. "I am twenty-two years old with no money, no family, and no talents. If I were clever like you, then I would have nothing to fear. I could obtain a post as governess in a good family. Unfortunately, I cannot draw, or play the pianoforte, or sing, and those are the accomplishments that governesses are supposed to teach their charges. So I must go to France as a servant."

"Surely Miss Turnbull has no objection to your remaining here? You make yourself so useful."

"For my board and lodging and a small dress allowance." Anna grimaced ruefully. "Miss Turnbull has been very generous to me, but it cannot alter the fact that I'm a charity pupil. *Was* a charity pupil! Now I'm a—I am not certain what I am. I only know that if I don't accept this situation I will spend the rest of my life here, helping out where I can and never seeing anything or going anywhere."

"You are so pretty," Anne said, regarding the delicate features and long-lashed blue eyes. "You ought to be married."

"With no dowry at all," Anna said, "my chances are slim. If I remain here my chances are negligible. The only gentleman we ever see is an occasional embarrassed father or elder brother."

"Has no offer ever been made to trace your relatives?"

"I believe that in the beginning one or two half-hearted attempts were made, but the orphanage authorities have quite enough to do taking care of the children without making enquiries on their behalf. Most of them are there because they have no families, and such enquiries would be fruitless anyway. Apparently, I was found sitting in the gutter outside the home, bawling my head off. There was a note pinned to me giving my name and date of birth and a locket round my neck. You've seen it."

"Let me see it again."

"It's just a gold locket." Anna reached into the neck of her dress and pulled it out. "It opens, but there was never anything inside it."

The locket had three tiny jewels set within an engraved triangle. Anne nodded as she bent closer to examine it.

"As you say, it's a locket—but surely worth something if it's gold."

"Not an enormous amount, and the stones are too tiny to be valuable. The matron gave it to me when I came here."

She had been twelve then, the age at which inmates were usually sent out into service or apprenticed somewhere. Anna had been fortunate. A lively, pretty child, she had been noticed by Miss Turnbull, who had come seeking a maidservant.

"You must have been delighted to leave the orphanage," Anne said with sympathy.

"Oh, it was not such a dreadful place," Anna assured her. "The matron was a good woman, and then I was a sweet-tempered child, so they tell me. You know when I was found? I could only say one or two words, and they sounded like French ones, so perhaps I have foreign blood. Not that it makes much difference now, but it would be interesting to find out."

"Is that why you are really going to France?" Anne enquired with interest.

"Heavens, no!" Anna laughed, her melancholy vanishing. "I merely want to see more of the world than this bit of Devonshire, and when Felice left—"

"Was requested to leave, because she did something very shocking with the gardener's boy."

"I wonder what it was. I suspect she allowed him to kiss her. Anyway, Felice's father has a cousin who requires a sewing woman. They want an English girl who will help the children in the family to improve their English conversation. They are between governesses or something. So they wrote to Miss Turnbull who thought that I might enjoy the change."

"Do you think you will?" Anne asked curiously.

"It will be a change of servitude at least." Anna's pretty face clouded again. "I will be working in a different place, that's all. If I am exceedingly fortunate one of the under-footmen will fall in love with me and not mind that I have no dowry, but I don't believe anything will happen at all. After a few months, they will discover how inefficient I am, and I will return here. It must be so exciting to be you on the verge of your first season."

"You may take my place any time you choose," Anne retorted. "At least as sewing maid you will be earning some money—"

"The equivalent of sixteen pounds a year."

"—and you are bound to have some time to yourself in a large household. I would give a deal to be in your situation during the next two or three months."

She stopped short, staring at her friend, her mouth

slightly open as if she had just tasted a new and unfamiliar idea.

"What is it?" Anna asked.

"What I just said," Anne said slowly. "I wish to change places with you for a while, and you wish to change places with me."

"So?"

"So what is to prevent us from doing just that?"

"You are funning! You cannot possibly be serious!"

"I am entirely serious." Anne had lowered her voice, but her grey eyes were shining. "I am to go to Yorkshire to live with an uncle I have not seen since I was ten years old, and that was the sole occasion on which we did meet. He never visited us when my father was alive, and he has more or less ignored my existence ever since. If you were to travel up to Yorkshire in my stead he would never know the difference. And you have not been personally interviewed for the situation you are taking in France, so I could travel there as you."

"Felice's father—"

"Felice and her family live in Toulouse. They are in the highest degree unlikely to be visiting Paris while you are there. It would only be for two or three months, time for you to get a taste of the social life you crave, and for me to—to have some time to myself." Not even to Anna had she confided any word of the book.

"It's one of the most madcap schemes ever devised," Anna said. "We don't even look alike!"

"Fair hair often darkens slightly as one grows older," Anne said. "The people to whom you are going have no physical description of you, have they? Our initials are the same and we can simple exchange our personal possessions—even garments if you like, for we are the same size. I am to have new clothes bought for me when I go to Yorkshire. Nobody will discover the difference."

"For you there would be no difficulty," Anna objected, "because you'd be an employee, and an orphan too. But I would be expected to know something about your family—if I were you, I mean. I'd be bound to make some terrible mistake and be exposed as an impostor."

"There's nothing to tell about the Sinclairs that we haven't talked about before," Anne reassured her. "My father was the elder son and he quarrelled with my grandfather—I believe my mother was considered an unsuitable match. My uncle took grandfather's side in the quarrel. Then grandfather died, and my mother died when I was born. Uncle Buckfast went up to Yorkshire. He came down after my father was killed riding, and brought me to Turnbull Academy."

"I remember your coming—not the actual night you arrived but the next morning. You were wearing a black dress, and you were so pale you looked like a piece of wax."

"And I considered you to be terribly grown-up." Anne smiled. In the years since, it seemed to her that she had caught up. Anna, enclosed first in the orphanage and then at the school, had remained young for her age. Yet Anne felt herself to be mature for eighteen. Perhaps it was because she had the keener mind and the knowledge at the back of it that she was rich.

"There is something you haven't considered," Anna said. "We cannot change places forever."

"I don't wish it. For two or three months only, to give you a taste of society—why, during that period someone might fall so much in love with you that he would find it romantic when your identity was revealed."

"I doubt your uncle would find it so very romantic,"

Anna said dryly. "He'd likely have me hauled before the magistrates for fraud."

"Not when you explained that I had persuaded you to it. He would be such a laughingstock among his neighbours that he'd hesitate about making it more public." Anne paused, then said, "Have I persuaded you to it?"

"It's tempting." The blue eyes were dancing. "But what would happen to me? Even if I was not accused publicly I would find it impossible to get a situation."

"Then I would insist upon engaging you as my companion," Anne said airily. "However, I am certain that someone will find you so irresistible that he will insist upon marrying you when the truth is known."

"If it might be contrived—" Anna had begun to shred the vine leaves again.

"Of course it can be!" Anne sprang up and began to pace the mosaic floor of the little pavilion. "We both travel to Plymouth. We shall contrive it so that we travel together on the same day. Then Miss Turnbull will not send another of the mistresses with me to make sure I get on the right coach for London. At Plymouth, we will exchange luggage, and you will take the London stage, and I will take ship for France!"

"Miss Turnbull acquired a passport for me."

"You must remember to give it to me before we part, and your boat ticket, too. You will land at Le Havre, or I will land at Le Havre, and then take a stage to—where is it these people live?"

"The Château de la Nuit, just outside Paris."

"Chateau of the Night! That sounds marvellously romantical. There must be a story attached to it. Well, I shall find it out when I arrive."

"But to travel alone in a foreign land—" Anna began nervously.

"My French is excellent, and I am as capable as you

of climbing aboard a stage." Anne whirled on her heel, her face flushing. "My journey will be shorter than yours anyway."

"But your uncle will doubtless send a servant to London to meet the Plymouth coach, to ensure you company for the rest of the way."

"And you will be the one whom the servant bears company," Anne said. "Of course it is possible that my uncle will send nobody at all. He has never yet displayed the slightest care for my convenience."

"Is it mainly to give Lord Sinclair a set down that you are doing this?" Anna asked abruptly.

"I hope my nature is not so disagreeable," Anne said, colouring up. "I confess I shall relish seeing him embarrassed, but it is entirely his own fault for being so high-handed. However, it is not only that. I promise you, I want very much to be able to prove to myself that I am not a foolish schoolgirl to be ordered about, and I do need some time for a—a private project I have in mind. And you would welcome an opportunity to attend balls and routs, would you not?"

"If you are sure there will be no lasting harm?" Anna said. She was weakening fast, as she always did when the younger girl set her mind upon something. But their scrapes in the past had been so mild as to go almost unnoticed. A paddle in the river one afternoon when the sun was scorching, ratafia, and a thimbleful of sherry eaten and drunk at midnight on Hallowe'en. Anna had not attended any classes for nearly six years, but was expected to render herself generally useful about the place. Their friendship had arisen out of a shared loneliness and had blossomed during the holidays, when most of the other pupils returned to their homes.

Miss Turnbull had noticed it, as she noticed everything, but had done nothing to discourage it. Anna Sayle, for all the lowliness of her background, had the instincts of a gentlewoman. The girl probably came of good stock, even if it was by way of the bend sinister. Anne Sinclair was often too intense and serious for a young girl, and would benefit from the other's more ebullient nature. Their paths would undoubtedly separate when Anne had finished her schooling. Had the principal had the faintest inkling of the scheme now being hatched, she would have been appalled.

Glancing through her parlour window as she rose from the reply she had just penned to Lord Sinclair, she saw the two girls walking along the path together, heads bent in conversation. She would miss them both, she admitted. It was not her habit to allow herself favourites among girls who were, after all, entrusted to her for only a limited period, but these two had grown up under her supervision.

She would have been quite content to have Anna stay on, but she had not stood in the way of the girl's desire to seek a situation elsewhere, and, if she were unhappy in France, she could always return. Anne Sinclair's destiny lay in another sphere. She would have her season and almost certainly be married.

"I do hope," Miss Turnbull murmured to herself, "that the child is not hoping for a Byronic husband, for she is doomed to disappointment."

She wondered if Anne would continue to hide her surreptitious purchase, the book of Lord Byron's poems that the headmistress knew very well she had, when she reached Yorkshire or if she would shock the high-handed Lord Sinclair by reading it openly. Some undeveloped sense of mischief in the principal's staid nature rather hoped the girl would choose the latter course.

I
Anne

=1=

MISS TURNBULL HAD spoken to both the young ladies separately on the eve of their departure.

"Miss Sinclair, I have the final details of your travelling times from your uncle. The London stage departs at seven in the morning, so it will be necessary for you to leave here shortly after five. Hodge will drive you and Miss Sayle to the stage. Miss Sayle's boat does not leave until eight, so there will be time for her to see you onto the coach. You will be met at London by a Dorcas Grant. She is one of the servants from Sinclair House and has been chosen by your uncle to act as your personal maid. You will have an overnight stay in London, but she has all the details of that. I do trust that is clear. I must confess to some trepidation at the necessity of sending you unescorted during the first part of your journey. However I am certain you will conduct yourself with the decorum proper to a young lady of your station."

"Yes, ma'am."

"I shall be sorry to lose you, my dear." The older woman's manner had perceptibly warmed. "You have been an excellent pupil. Had fate decreed it, you would have made a splendid governess. Fortunately, it will never be necessary for you to earn your own living, but I hope you will continue to read, even to study a little, after you are married, provided your husband is agreeable."

"I shall take care to choose one who is," Anne said with spirit.

"I fancy that in that matter you must be prepared to accept your uncle's guidance," Miss Turnbull said.

"I won't marry someone I dislike merely to please my uncle," Anne began, then recalling she would not be the one at whose head some socially acceptable bridegroom was thrown, added hastily, "But I am sure he would not force me to it."

"Merely endeavour to resist any temptation to wilfulness." Miss Turnbull clasped Anne's hand in her own. "I flatter myself that Lord Sinclair may well be pleased when he has formed an estimate of your character. I hope also you will write to assure me of your safe arrival."

"Of course, ma'am."

The letter, already written in the assumption that the journey would be without incident, reposed at the bottom of Anna's trunk, and she herself had a similar letter, penned by Anna, tucked into the portmanteau in which her friend's more modest wardrobe was packed. One could only trust that the ship would not be sunk nor the carriage overturn during their respective journeys.

"Then I advise you to retire. You have a long journey ahead of you," Miss Turnbull said. "I will rise early in order to bid both of you a final farewell."

She briefly embraced her pupil and heaved a sigh as Anne closed the door gently behind her. A pleasant girl with an intelligent mind! It was a pity that her originality would have to be stifled beneath layers of convention. Only the very poor or the very old could be allowed eccentricity.

Towards Anna, whom she saw next, her manner was subtly altered. Though she had always treated her more as pupil than servant, the fact remained that the young woman's destiny would be very different from that of the rich Miss Sinclair.

"You will see Miss Sinclair onto the stage and then go at once to the Hoe," she instructed. "The *Lafayette* sails at eight. I have your ticket here. When you reach Le Havre, you are to take the next stage to Paris. The baron and his wife have sent word that the porter will be awake to let you in should your time of arrival be delayed until very late. Your actual duties are not very clearly defined. It is possible you will find yourself with some leisure time on your hands, which I trust you will employ profitably. There are some very fine galleries and museums in the capital." She broke off, reflecting with her usual good sense that as Anna had shown no propensity for any intellectual pursuits up to now she was not likely to begin once she had crossed the Channel.

"Yes, ma'am," Anna said. Her tone was meek, but her expression was lively.

Her face betrayed her mood of the moment too clearly, the other thought, and blamed herself for not having succeeded in training the girl to wear the impassive mask of the discreet servant.

"You may find your position in the Lanuit household something different from what it has been here," she said tactfully. "One hopes that, since the Revolution and the war, domestics are treated with more humanity, and the letter I received from the baron was exceedingly civil, but you must not expect the laxity you have enjoyed at Turnbull Academy."

"I will not," Anna said, her voice still meek, her eyes still dancing.

She was a remarkably pretty girl, the principal thought. Her complexion was smooth as a petal, her nose short and straight, her mouth rosy above a round chin. Her brown hair had red and goldish lights in it, and curled naturally without the aid of tongs or papers.

"There is another matter." Miss Turnbull hesitated. "You have been endowed by Nature with considerable beauty—an outward beauty, it's true, which will not endure as long as the inner loveliness of soul which I trust you also possess. Up to now, you have led an exceedingly sheltered life. But you are going into a strange household in a foreign country where it is possible others may seek to take advantage of that innocence and inexperience. I am certain you will conduct yourself at all times in a manner that reflects credit upon your training."

"I will not allow myself to be seduced," Anna said with the disconcerting bluntness that occasionally characterised her speech.

"One trusts," the other said dryly, "the temptation will not arise. Remember that should the post not be to your liking you are welcome to return."

"Thank you, ma'am. I am truly most grateful for your kindness to me," Anna said.

One hoped that both the girls would prosper. In the chill dawn of the following day, Miss Turnbull, as neat at that early hour as if she were greeting the parents of prospective pupils, stood on the front step and raised a hand in farewell to the old, slightly shabby coach that remained from her father's day. Hodge, also a relic from her youth, would deliver his charges and was under strict orders to return as soon as he had watered the horses. In his later years he had become a little too enamoured of tavern fare; a fault from which Miss Turnbull hoped to wean him.

During the hour-and-a-half drive, the two girls said

very little. They were not anxious for Hodge to overhear any fragment of betraying conversation, and each was busy with her own thoughts. Anna, having been persuaded, was now looking forward eagerly to the thrill of an introduction to the high society from which her circumstances had, so far, debarred her. Anne, having initiated the scheme, was pensive for a different reason. It was one thing to plan a rebellion, but actually carrying it out gave her an unwontedly nervous feeling in the pit of her stomach. Yet, given the choice, she would not have drawn back. The impersonation would not hurt anybody, and if Lord Buckfast Sinclair were socially embarrassed by it, she was inclined to think that he deserved it.

Plymouth was well astir when they reached it, shops opening, apprentices with leather aprons hurrying to their benches, mobcapped housewives leaning from upper windows to call to their neighbours, drayhorses making their slow, lumbering way over the cobbles. The stagecoach was already being loaded, and intending passengers stood about stamping their feet, exchanging last minute trivialities with their friends and blowing on their fingers, for the early mornings still nipped.

The girls feared that Hodge might take Miss Turnbull's instructions so literally as to insist on seeing Anne into the coach and Anna aboard the Channel ferry, but fortunately he had already marked with his eye a certain hostelry where he could snatch a quick bite and a pint of porter without being unduly late returning to the academy and, having unloaded the baggage and touched his forelock several times, he clambered up to the driving seat again and drove off.

Anne, the last minute twinges of apprehension becoming definite cowardice, glanced at the other girl.

"You are absolutely certain that you're willing to go through with this?"

"I haven't the faintest intention of letting you down by breaking my word," Anna said. "To be honest, I am truly beginning to relish the adventure."

"Oh, so am I!" Anne sounded more enthusiastic than she felt. "Now we must get my—that is to say 'your' luggage aboard the stage."

"And here are the passport and ticket—oh! and the letter from the baron! How will you get to the ferry?"

"There are some gigs for hire over there. I shall contrive very well. You will write to me post-haste if any emergency occurs?"

"I promise." Anna embraced the younger girl, then said, "Wait! I almost forgot." She put her hands to her neck and unclasped the thin gold chain on which the locket hung. "Now that you are Anna Sayle, you must wear this."

"I couldn't possibly—it's the only jewel you have," Anne protested.

"Wear it beneath your bodice as a token of our friendship." Anna pressed it upon her.

"Which will continue long after this adventure is concluded." Anne tucked the jewel under the high neckline of the grey dress she had chosen to wear. More plainly cut than any of her garments, it had been dubbed by both of them as very suitable for a sewing maid.

"Ladies! Which of your is travelling to London?" The stagecoach driver, resplendent in a three-tiered greatcoat and cocked hat, approached them genially.

"Miss Sinclair." Anne indicated Anna. "Hers are the cases of dark blue leather. She is to be met at London."

"Right you are, Miss!" The coachman summoned his assistant with a lordly gesture and turned to help Anna up the high step into the interior. Other passengers were entering, those gentlemen who were spry and impoverished enough to ride outside, clambering up to the top where they would cling to the bar at the side and inform one another the view was vastly superior from this vantage point.

"Do take care!" Anne mouthed, standing back as steps were folded, doors slammed, harness tightened. The horses, fresh and eager to be off, strained at their bits, the lead pair jerking away from the restraining hand of the ostler. Anna's piquant face, framed in a straw bonnet, appeared briefly at the window. Then the ostler handed up the reins, the driver lifted the horn to his lips and blew the long note of beginning, and the team sprang forward, the stage rocking as it rumbled over the cobbles. Several small boys, shirts hanging out of their breeches, clung to the back guard rail, to the imminent peril of life and limb, until the rapidly increasing speed forced them to let go, and the stage vanished in a cloud of white dust at the bend in the road.

Anne, left with her friend's scantier and shabbier luggage, shook off a sudden feeling of loneliness and beckoned one of the gig drivers.

"I have to board the *Lafayette*, which casts off in an hour," she said crisply. "Can you take me to the quayside?"

"Yes, Miss." He was clearly eager for custom, promptly shouldering the trunk and portmanteau, and helping her up to the passenger seat. "Going to France then?"

"To Paris. I have a situation there."

"A situation?" His expression was so surprised that she wondered if he had possibly recognised her from some previous chaperoned visit. "Starting out in style, ain't we, Miss?"

His sideways glance and the slow lowering of his

eyelid clarified matters. Working girls did not airily hire a gig to drive them a short distance. They paid a man to carry the heavy bags and themselves trudged behind on foot.

"Beginning as I hope to go on," she said. "I'm going to work for a baron."

"I thought all of them French nobs had their heads chopped off long since."

"Some of them didn't."

"Them that wasn't killed at Trafalgar and Waterloo got what was left, I daresay," he nodded. "Well, now that Boney's locked up tight on St. Helena, I reckon it's safe enough to travel in France. Will you be eating snails and frog's legs?"

"Not," said Anne with a slight shudder, "if I can avoid it."

"Well, it takes all sorts," the driver said with an air of having discovered some great original truth. "Me, I'd not stir out of England for all that we've a mad King and a Regent who cannot live in peace with his wife. It's to be hoped the Princess Charlotte brings us an heir. There's the *Lafayette*, Miss! Will you be going steerage?"

"No, indeed," Anne began haughtily, adding truthfully, but hastily, "The baron reserved me a place in one of the cabins."

"Sounds like a decent sort."

They had reached the long quayside with the tall-masted ships bobbing at anchor, their sails white crests above the slap-slap of the grey-green water. Smaller vessels, like bridesmaids, fluttered up and down the narrow aisles between. There was a tang of salt and tar and drying hemp and nets being landed filled with wriggling silver-grey fish at one end of the quay.

"How much?" Anne felt for her purse.

"Have this one as a farewell gift from me," the driver said. "You don't want to go wasting your money on gigs, you know. Like as not you'll be cheated the minute you set foot on French soil! I'll find a lad to carry your bags!"

"That's very kind of you," Anne said as she stepped down.

"Glad to lend a hand to a fellow mortal," he said loftily. "Mind, if you'd been a real lady I'd have charged double! Hey, you! here's a halfpenny. Take this lot aboard the *Lafayette* and don't drop 'em, or I'll tell the pressgang what you look like! I wish you luck, Miss. I really do."

Anne shook hands cordially and followed the boy up the gangplank, feeling cheered by the brief encounter. It was, after all, exciting to be an independent female embarking on her first voyage to foreign parts. She showed her passport and ticket to the official at the head of the gangway and was soon looking in some dismay round a tiny cabin already occupied by two voluble matrons who broke off their chatter to glare at her icily for a second and then, turning their backs, continued what sounded like a character assassination of everybody with whom they were acquainted.

Anne heaved her bags onto the only vacant bunk and sat down. She would have liked to go on deck to see the vessel cast off, but the remote possibility that Hodge might have taken it into his head to come down and wave farewell to Anna held her in her place. When the first lurch of the ship told her they had cleared the harbour, she left her seat and went out to the deck.

The rail was crowded with passengers, and there was a babble of voices in a mixture of English and French. French had been one of her strongest subjects at school but, listening to the swift, slurred patter, she realised it would take her some time before she was accustomed to the colloquialisms of the native born. Meanwhile she wedged herself in a corner, watching the sails billow over her head, the water change to a deeper blue as the harbour receded, and the sun shine more brilliantly.

Those passengers who had not secured cabin places were making themselves as comfortable as possible on upturned suitcases. High in the rigging, she could see sailors bracing their bare feet against the tarred ropes. Near her feet, a couple of small children were playing some guessing game or other while their mother, swathed in shawls, constantly admonished them not to lean over the side.

"Which they had not thought of doing until their mama warned them against it," said an amused voice at her elbow. The voice spoke English with only the slightest of accents and issued from a slim good-looking young man with fair curly hair who had come to lean on the rail next to her.

Anne smiled without speaking. One did not enter into conversation with gentlemen to whom one had not been introduced.

The newcomer seemed unaware of the social niceties however, continuing easily, "I noticed that you were alone, and as I am alone too, it is pleasant to strike up a conversation. I have spent so much time aboard ship recently that I can no longer go into raptures about the beauties of sea and sky."

"Oh?" Her natural curiosity overcoming her, Anne sent him a questioning look.

"I'm returning home from Québec," he volunteered. " 'Home' being France. I couldn't obtain a direct passage and, as I'd business in England anyway, I broke up my journey for a month. Oh, my name is

Edouard de Reynard. I should have told you that in the beginning."

"Anna Sayle." She shook hands.

"English, of course. Only an English lady would have the courage to travel alone."

"I am going to a situation in Paris," she informed him.

"A situation? Ah, I thought—"

"That I was travelling on pleasure? No, I am a working woman." She gripped the rail as the wind caught the sails and the vessel, hesitating on the crest of a billow, dipped down sharply.

"There is a small dining area where one may purchase light refreshments." His hand was under her elbow, steadying her. "May I offer my escort there? We are making unusual speed, I think, and it will be far better for you to sit nearer the centre of the vessel and eat something. It is a precaution against the *mal-de-mer*."

"I do not," said Anne, who was beginning to feel slightly queasy, "intend to suffer from *mal-de-mer*."

"In that case we must take the precaution I advocated. It is also some time since I took any breakfast."

There was no point in arguing. Anne allowed herself to be led to the dining salon where, seated at a round table with grooves to hold utensils, she began to feel decidedly better.

"Croissants, honey, coffee and apple jelly—all very light and wholesome. You will feel better when you have eaten." He gave the order to a steward.

"I do not actually feel so unwell," Anne confessed. "However this is my first sea voyage."

"Your first visit then to France? It is my second. My parents emigrated to Canada when I was only a few months old, because of the political situation. I am returning for the first time. I was curious about the Old World of which my parents so often talk." He passed her a croissant.

"You were in London?"

"My mother's brother fled to London. He also never returned, being unalterably opposed to the ambitions of Bonaparte. He died a year ago, leaving me a small property he still retained on the outskirts of Paris. His London lawyers assure me it will be easy to sell, but I decided to visit it myself before giving definite instructions one way or the other."

"You have a title then, with a 'de' in your name?"

"My uncle was a count, which means that my father inherited the title. He left his London house to charity—but, in the New World, we do not set so much store by title, unless one is a Prince of the Blood or its equivalent."

"And you are not."

"By profession I am a physician." He smiled at her expression. "Did you imagine all physicians are past forty with black beards and solemn expressions? I am six-and-twenty and have been qualified for eighteen months. I hope to return to Québec and buy myself a practice."

"I applaud your industry, sir." Anne raised her coffee cup.

"But not my talking incessantly about myself! Do you go as a governess?"

"A sewing maid, but I am to give some lessons in English conversation, I believe. To the Baron Lanuit?"

"The name is not familiar." He shook his head. "My uncle's house—my house now—is in the Rue St. Jacques. I am informed by the lawyers that it is still in good repair. I shall remain there for a few weeks at least."

He gave her a faintly expectant look, no doubt

hoping that she would disclose her destination. Anne, although she was satisfied that he was an amiable and respectable young man whose slight unconventionality arose from his having been reared in a more informal society, maintained a discreet silence. It was no part of her plan to allow herself to become entangled in even a casual friendship.

Edouard de Reynard, however, appeared content to continue chatting in desultory fashion about himself. His father, he told her, had ceded his own right of inheritance to his only son and taken pleasure in running a farm on the outskirts of Québec.

"In theory he has always embraced Republican ideals, but that would have availed him nothing during the Terror, and he refused to return and live under the rule of an upstart. Now he and mother are too set in their ways. He retains French customs and attitudes but regards himself as a Canadian now—as I do myself. I look forward to hanging out my shingle. I believe that during this century medicine will make tremendous strides forward. There is much to be learned."

Anne, sipping a second cup of coffee, listened with growing sympathy. This young man might have chosen to return to France and lead an idle, frivolous existence, but he had not permitted his inheritance to deflect him from his chosen ambitions.

"Are you being met at Le Havre?" he broke off to enquire.

"I am to take the Paris stage. My employer's estate is some miles before the city, so I will be alighting before the final stop."

"It will be very late when you arrive."

"I understand someone will be there to admit me and show me to my room."

"I intend to bespeak a nights lodging at Le Havre

and continue my journey by daylight. I will be sorry not to have the pleasure of your company for the last part of the journey."

"I doubt if I will be much company," Anne said. "I have a feeling I will sleep the last part of the journey away."

"You wish to retire?"

"Not in the least," she assured him. "Thanks to your advice the threat of *mal-de-mer* has been routed, and I would like to go on deck again and enjoy some of the benefits of the sea air."

"Which I, as a physician, heartily recommend," he told her.

The voyage, which might have proved tedious by herself, sped by in an agreeable fashion. The physician—"I prefer my title of doctor to any my uncle bequeathed me, since I earned it for myself"—secured two deck chairs in a sheltered spot where she was able to divide her attention between the water rushing past and his slightly too graphic accounts of his experiences when walking the wards in a Québec hospital.

When the French coastline hove into view she sat up eagerly, her langour vanishing.

"If you will permit me, I will see you and your luggage safely aboard the coach," Edouard de Reynard said. "Unless you have reserved a seat in advance, it may be difficult to secure a place."

"That's very civil of you," Anne said gratefully. Her path, which she had expected to be rocky, was being smoothed out for her every step of the way.

The bustle of disembarkation was slightly bewildering. She was glad of escort, as a porter was summoned to carry her luggage to the waiting stage and another official, speaking French at this side of the Channel, checked and stamped her passport.

"I wish you a pleasant stay in our country, Mademoiselle Sayle," he said, saluting as he returned it to her.

Edouard de Reynard, who had left her side for a few moments, returned with the ticket and the small stock of francs into which he had changed the sovereigns with which she had entrusted him.

"You have a window seat in the stage, and the remainder is yours. I bought some food for you to eat on the journey since there are no halts long enough for a meal."

The square box contained fruit and rolls and some cheese. Anne smilingly thanked him, having the tact not to offer to pay.

"I hope our paths cross again, Miss Sayle." He took her proferred hand and shook it in the English style. "I wish you the best of good fortune."

"And I you, sir."

Climbing up into the interior, she settled herself with the box on her knee. Though the *Lafayette* had made almost record time and it was still light, it would be midnight before she reached her destination, and it seemed a very long time since she had eaten in the dining salon. The sea air, combined with the early rising, had also made her sleepy.

She had never gone by stage before and, before the first hour was up, she was pitying Anna, whose overland journey would take so much longer. The constant bumping and swaying, the close proximity of the other passengers, the confinement of closed windows and a flat, featureless landscape over which twilight began to steal, combined to make her feel wretched. She leaned her head back and dozed fitfully, aware of the conversation of the other passengers, which she was not alert enough to translate, then was jerked fully awake when they stopped to change horses.

There was scarcely time for her to stretch her legs in the cobbled yard of the posting inn before they were being summoned back. She opened the box and forced herself to nibble some of the fruit and bread. A buxom woman seated opposite her poured some wine from a bottle into a little cup and offered it to her. She accepted it and offered in return an apple from the box. The repast finished, she smiled wordlessly at the woman, then closed her eyes and drifted into sleep again.

It was dark when she was woken by the sound of a name being called at the window. The coach had stopped, and the other occupants were looking enquiringly at one another.

"Mademoiselle Sayle? Sayle?" The coachman's face was round and red.

"Yes? Yes, I am Mademoiselle Sayle." She struggled to sit upright.

"You said the halt before Paris?"

"Yes. Yes, this is it." She was helped down into the road and her bags handed down to her.

A moment later the stage had rolled on, and she stood, stiff with cramp and slightly dizzy from waking up too fast. The highway was deserted, and only an avenue of trees swayed and rustled in the night wind beyond high iron gates.

As she stood there uncertainly a head was stuck out from the window of a small building within the gates, and a voice demanded, "Mademoiselle Sayle?"

"Yes. *Oui. C'est moi.*" She moved towards the gates.

The head vanished and a man, elderly, to judge from his gait, came forward, opened a small gate within the large ones and stepped through, peering at her bags.

"Take one up to the house, and I'll bring the rest in the morning," he began.

From behind the gates a voice said loudly, "You'll bring them all up now, you lazy devil, or I'll flog the skin from your shoulders! Mademoiselle, step inside and follow me."

The figure on horseback, who had risen up as if out of the ground, wheeled about and trotted up the avenue at the far end of which Anne could discern a large building with, here and there, a light burning in a window.

"Devil himself!" the porter muttered. "Takes one to know one!"

Anne, obedient to the rider's commands, stepped through the gate and set off up the avenue in the wake of the departing hoofbeats. Behind her she could hear the porter's continuing monologue as he lugged the bags through the aperture.

The avenue was much longer than she had realised and, as she approached, the house was much larger. She stumbled once or twice through sheer fatigue and felt a decided relief when she saw the front door open at the top of a flight of steps. At each side of the door a terrace stretched dimly to left and right.

The man on the horse sat in the saddle and looked down at her as she reached the foot of the steps.

"So you're the English mademoiselle!" he exclaimed.

"Yes, sir. I am Anna Sayle." She was already becoming accustomed to the name, she thought. Very soon she would respond automatically when it was called.

"Come to mend our clothes and teach us all to speak the English tongue!"

"I hope so, sir."

"Right." He shrugged, waving his hand towards the

steps. "Across the hall, first door on the right, and follow your nose up the stairs."

"I am grateful," she said, stung, "for your precise directions, sir."

"Someone put your name on the door. There's a lamp in the hall. I'd escort you myself save that I've other matters to attend."

He flicked the reins and bounded into the darkness, leaving her with an impression of a mocking and contemptuous manner designed to put her firmly in her place. The great difficulty was that she was already having trouble remembering where her place was supposed to be.

The hall was immense, caverns of gloom interrupted by low burning lamps that scarcely began to pierce the dark. She took up one of the lamps, turning the wick higher. Over her head was a painted ceiling and beneath her feet a marble floor. There were arched doorways all round, encircled with wreaths of gold leaf.

The first door on the right opened onto a long corridor with windows overlooking the terrace at one side and a row of similarly arched and wreathed doors on the other. At the far end a narrow staircase stretched up into darkness. As Anne walked towards it her shoes struck hollow echoes from the cold marble.

She had reached the top of the staircase when she heard the mumbling of the porter, balancing the few pieces of luggage as if they weighed a ton. He passed her without glancing in her direction, opened a door farther down the corridor beyond the landing, dropped the bags with a decided thud, and came out, again passing without a word.

"And a pleasant good-night to you!" Anne said loudly in her carefully precise French and went on to the open door. A notice with her name crayoned on it in red hung on the door handle. Within the room the ashes of a dying fire glowed in the hearth, but the bed was made, there was a thick carpet on the floor, and at that moment she was too weary to trouble her head over the lack of welcome.

— 2 —

SHE WOKE TO broad daylight and whispering voices. Opening her eyes, she looked straight at two small children who stood at the side of the bed and regarded her with intense curiosity. The boy, who was clearly the elder, was about nine, his black hair cut in page boy fashion, his nankeen breeches and satin tunic decidedly grubby. Clutching his hand and wearing an equally soiled petticoat was a small girl who peered through a tangled mop of curls.

"Good-morning." Anne sat up, blinking the last vestiges of sleep out of her eyes.

The boy bent and whispered to the girl, who promptly giggled and stuck out her tongue as far as it would go.

"Is that a new form of greeting?" Anne spoke in French.

"My sister is not greeting," the boy said. "She wants you to depart."

"As this is my room it is for you to depart," Anne told him. "I suppose you are the ploughboy's children?"

"We are the children of the Baron Lanuit." The boy raised his head haughtily.

"The badly behaved children of the Baron Lanuit," Anne corrected calmly.

"It is not for an English mademoiselle to teach us good manners," he scowled.

"It should not be necessary," she agreed.

The children regarded her suspiciously. Then the boy said, by way of making a great concession, "I am Gaston Lanuit and this is Justine. I am nine and she is six."

"And the baron is your father." She tried to keep the disapproval out of her voice, but the boy flushed as he answered,

"We choose to be like this."

"How very foolish of you." Anne pushed back the covers and swung her feet over the side of the bed. "I feel more comfortable when I am clean and tidy myself."

"You are Anna Sayle?"

"You may call me Anna, if you wish," she said.

"We don't wish to call you anything," Gaston said. "We don't want any more governesses."

"I don't want to be your governess either," Anne told him. "Fortunately I am here only to sew your clothes and to speak English with you."

"We don't wish to speak English."

"Very well! Remain ignorant if you choose. It will mean less work for me, and I suspect that you are not clever enough to learn it anyway."

"We speak it very beautifully when we choose," he said slowly in English, "but we do not choose."

"As you wish." Assuming indifference she nodded towards the door. "You may leave me now while I make my toilet."

If they had refused, she would have been uncertain what to do, but to her relief they went, pausing at the door to give her a last, considering look.

The water in the ewer was stone cold, but the

iciness refreshed her. She unpacked Anna's—she must learn to think of them as her own—clothes, hung them in the cavernous wardrobe, and put on a brown dress with white yoke and cuffs. Her hair was dropping out of curl and was too short to braid properly, so she combed it back and secured it in a small knot. The severity of the gown and hairstyle made her look nearer the twenty-two years she was supposed to be, and, when she beheld her reflection in the mirror, she thought, with a rueful quirk of the lips, that it was unlikely anyone, even an under-footman, would fall in love with her.

She opened the door and went out into the corridor. From somewhere near at hand, she fancied she could hear a giggle, but she ignored it and walked on down the stairs along the corridor and into the vast entrance hall.

By daylight, she could see it clearly, the unwashed marble, the flaking gold leaf, the dingy windows. The chateau obviously had two wings sweeping back from the main hall. Her room was probably in the servants' wing, which meant the family sleeping quarters would be at the other side. The main door stood open, and she walked out, stood at the top of the steps, and looked down the avenue of elm trees to the tiny lodge at the gates. The sunshine flooding everything with gold also revealed the broken flower pots along the edge of the terrace. The whole place reminded her of a once great beauty, now grown shabby and neglected.

A figure hove into view at the end of the terrace. She recognised the broad shoulders and carriage of the black head before he was close enough for her to see his features. Shadowed the previous night, they were now revealed as heavily handsome in a mocking, saturnine fashion. "Byronic," Anne thought, remembering to bob a curtsey as he reached her.

"Miss Sayle, good morning." His English was good, his accent slight.

"Good-morning, sir."

"You are surveying the beauties of the estate?" He raised an eyebrow.

"I was wondering where I could get something to eat," Anne said bluntly.

"If you require an English breakfast, you will have to cook it yourself. My wife generally has coffee and croissants at this hour," he returned, "so you had better come and make your bow to her. There will be leftovers, for she does not eat sufficient to satisfy a sparrow."

Without waiting for an answer, he turned and strode back along the terrace. As she had guessed, there was another wing of the building here. The baron went through a side door and up a winding flight of stairs, rapped at a door, and, opening it, said loudly in French, "Sophie, my dear, the English sewing maid is come, and nobody has yet troubled to feed her, it appears. Have you anything to spare for a starving foreigner?"

"She may have all of this," a voice answered fretfully. "It is abominably prepared!"

Anne, stepping into the long, low chamber, had to wait a moment before her eyes became accustomed to the dim light that filtered through the drawn shutters. The room seemed smaller than it actually was because it was crammed with furniture, tables crowded with ornaments jostled with spindly legged chairs, the walls were hung with dozens of pictures, and there was an overpowering reek of dust.

"Madame La Baronne." Reaching a sofa on which a woman reclined, Anne bobbed another curtsey.

"You are Mademoiselle Sayle? I was told you were expected." Sophie Lanuit's voice matched her surroundings. It was low and husky, each word drawled out as if unwillingly. "Please help yourself to what you want. We do not stand upon formality here."

At the side of the couch a small table bore a silver tray on which were coffee pot and cups, a jar of preserves, and some croissants.

"That's very kind of you, madame." Anne took the chair indicated by a languid hand and proceeded to help herself. "I had very little yesterday, as I was travelling."

"An abominable journey it must have been!" The baroness shuddered.

"It was a novel experience for me," Anne said cheerfully. "This is the first time I have been out of England."

"Mademoiselle Turnbull recommended you most highly." The pale face under its wealth of chestnut hair was briefly illuminated by a shaft of sunlight that pierced a gap in the shutters.

The baroness was in her late twenties, Anne realised. The face thus briefly revealed was startlingly white and drawn, the eyes dark circled, the mouth compressed.

"I am a sad invalid, I fear," she was continuing. "I do not have either will or energy to oversee the household as I might, and the servants are insufferably lazy."

"I have met your children, Madame," Anne said, pouring coffee into one of the clean cups. "Clean," she reflected, was a relative word. The most one could say was that it had not recently been drunk from.

"The children are young savages," the baron said. He was leaning against the wall, his arms folded.

"They are in need of a governess," Anne began, and was interrupted from the sofa.

"I will not have—I utterly refuse to have another governess here! They have all proved unsatisfactory, and a very bad influence on the children. Jean, I thought I made it clear—"

"No governesses." The baron's voice held a shrug.

"You were engaged as a sewing maid." His wife's voice was sharp. "You can sew?"

"Yes, Madame. Plain sewing and embroidery, but I understood I was also expected to give practice in English conversation."

"Oh, if you wish to do that, I have no objection." The white hand rose and fell. "But I will not have another governess in the household. You promised me, Jean."

"About my duties—" Anne began.

"Oh, you will have plenty to occupy your time," the baroness said. "There is always mending to be done, and then I have no objection to your speaking English with the children or lending a hand where you see it is needed. I am certain you will occupy yourself."

"Yes, Madame." Anne concealed her puzzlement. It looked as if she had been given carte blanche to arrange her time as she chose. She was determined that two or three hours a day would be devoted to her writing.

"Open the shutters a little," the husky voice commanded. "I wish to see you clearly."

Anne, obeying, wondered if her youthfulness would be too apparent. The baron had seen her in the full glare of day and seemed not to notice, but women were more perceptive. The heavily shadowed eyes that roved over her face however seemed indifferent.

"I am not much to look at," she said lightly, to hide her discomfort at being thus examined, "but I assure you my needlework is superior."

"You will do well enough," the baroness said. "Close the shutters again. The light is too strong."

"I will make myself familiar with the routine of the

household, draw up a timetable, and begin my duties first thing tomorrow morning." Anne spoke briskly, dipping a curtsey.

"As you please. I am sure you will be diligent." The languid hand waved her away as the slender figure sank back against the pillows.

"Routine, timetable, duties." The baron, following her down the stairs and onto the terrace, mocked her softly. "How very English you sound, Mademoiselle!"

"As my duties appear to be somewhat nebulous," she said primly, "I shall do my best to earn my salary as well as I can. I was to receive three months in advance?"

"So it was agreed." He brought some coins from his breast pocket and held out his hand, palm up. There was a decided glint in his brown eyes.

"I will receive my salary when you pay the rest of your household, and it can be properly entered in the books," she said.

"In that event, you may find yourself waiting for a very long time," he said. "I am notoriously slow at paying my servants."

"Which probably explains a great deal," Anne said tartly, before she could stop herself.

"For a serving maid, you have a remarkably literate vocabulary," he remarked.

"I was fortunate enough to receive a very good education from Miss Turnbull," she said quickly.

"I wonder you do not hire yourself out as a governess." He began to lay the coins out neatly on a nearby sill.

"I am not intellectual."

"And governesses are not, as you will have gathered, very popular round here. My wife is delicate and suffers from jealous fancies. It is, her physicians inform me, a symptom of her mania."

"With me," Anne said levelly, meeting the dark gaze, "she will not have to worry at all."

"As you say." His eyes swept over her, and then he bowed and strode off.

She moved to the sill and collected up the coins. This was a peculiar household, run-down and disorderly, with its cynical master and invalid mistress, its badly behaved children. Anna—the real Anna—would not have been able to cope. Within herself, she felt the response to a challenge.

The first thing to be done was to explore. So far she had not seen a single servant, but, even as that thought entered her mind, a girl with an apron round her waist came through the front door and began half-heartedly to sweep the steps.

"Excuse me!" Anne went towards her, seeing the girl hesitate, suspicion in her small blue eyes.

"Mademoiselle?" The servant leaned on her broom, not troubling to curtsey. Anne, who was about to rebuke her for it, remembered in time that sewing maids did not receive curtseys.

"The baron wishes me to go round the château and note what needs to be done," she said instead. "I would be grateful if you would accompany me."

"Me, Mademoiselle?" the girl gaped at her.

"If you would be so kind—? You have a name?"

"Berthe," the girl said. "You're the new—governess?"

"I have come to do the sewing and make myself generally useful," Anne said. "I am not a governess."

"Oh." Berthe, still looking bewildered, said, "The governess left six months back."

"Shall we begin in the main hall? I have been in the baroness's chamber."

"Her salon," Berthe said unexpectedly. "Her bedroom is next to it. She moves between the two."

Moves like some delicate creature in a green cage, Anne was surprised to find herself thinking.

"Where are the servants' quarters and the kitchens?" she said aloud. "Where are the other servants?"

"Here and there," Berthe said vaguely. "Cook is in the kitchen putting his feet up. Mathilde went to make the beds, I think. The men'll be in the stables, smoking their pipes till the baron's step is heard."

"We'd better start in the kitchen," Anne said. As she had guessed, the doors leading off the lower passage in the east wing gave onto a warren of servants' rooms, pantries, linen rooms, store cupboards, and, at the end of a steep flight of stairs a large basement kitchen, thick with soot and grease, where a large individual sat with his feet up on a stool, reading a newspaper.

"Monsieur le chef?" Anne spoke loudly.

The newspaper was lowered, and a dough pale face was raised to hers.

"I," said the large individual, "am Monsieur Louis."

"I am Mademoiselle Sayle." Anne drew a nervous breath and went on. "I wish to inspect the linen and the silver, all the closets. Who has the keys?"

"The governess had them. Are you the new governess?"

"I am not a governess," Anne repeated patiently. "I am here to do the sewing and to do whatever I think may be necessary for the smooth running of the household."

She was positive that she was exceeding her duties by claiming such sweeping responsibilities, but before any mending or stitching could be undertaken, it would do no harm to have a thorough cleaning. The thought of eating another meal prepared in this odiferous place sickened her.

At her side, Berthe suddenly volunteered, "The

keys are in the cupboard, Mademoiselle, but only the wine cellar is locked, and the baron keeps the key of that himself."

"Leave the wine cellar. You!" Glavanized by a rush of energy, Anne beckoned a lanky youth who had just slouched in.

"That's Philippe, the under-footman," Berthe said.

"The under—!" Anne choked back a laugh. Certainly there was no danger of her succumbing to the seductive fascination of this unprepossessing individual. "Well, I want this room and all the pantries scrubbed and all the dishes washed and the silver cleaned and the stale food thrown into bins and burned. You cannot expect Monsieur Louis to create meals fit for a family in this pigsty. Get the other men to help you."

"Are those the baron's orders?" the lanky Philippe asked doubtfully.

"Those are *my* orders!" Monsieur Louis cast aside the newspaper and rose with dignity that was truly majestic. "You will do my bidding! Go!"

Philippe left the kitchen with dispatch.

"Now I must inspect the bed linen," Anne said. "May I rely on you—?"

"The kitchens will sparkle," declared her unlikely ally. "Return later, Mademoiselle, and you will see."

"We will look over the rest of the chateau." Anne inclined her head and swept out.

At her heels Berthe said, her voice awed, "The last governess never went near the kitchens."

"I am not—never mind! We will take a look at what else needs to be done."

"It all needs doing," Berthe said, "but nobody ever troubles."

Perhaps that was what was wrong, Anne thought,

as they toiled from room to room. Many of the chambers had been unused for what was clearly a long time. They had a damp, musty smell, and the dust sheets shrouding the furniture were stained brown. Yet the rooms had been beautiful once, the ceilings gilded and painted with scenes from classical myth, the walls hung with silk, mirrors reflecting the light from a hundred candelabra.

"There must be fires lit and the windows opened, the floors waxed and drapes washed and ironed, the ornaments cleaned and some of the mirrors resilvered." She was rapping out her orders to an astonished Berthe, who trotted after her as if she were in a kind of spell.

"I can't keep it all in my head at once!" the girl wailed at last.

"Tomorrow morning we will go into every room and put up a list of what requires to be done in that particular chamber," Anne said, stopping short. "For today, it will be enough if the kitchen is cleaned so that a decent repast may be cooked. The baroness's croissants were stale this morning."

"Madame never notices," Berthe said.

"The baron cannot possibly be satisfied with such a state of affairs, surely?"

"The baron's not been home very often since the la—since the governess left."

"What was her name?" It was wrong to encourage servants' gossip, but she had no intention of asking the baron.

"Fräulein Schloss and, before that, there was Señorita Luisa Dios and before—"

"There have been a succession of governesses then?" Anne sat down on the nearest chair and stared at the girl.

"Until the baron wearies of them and pays them off," Berthe said.

"Did they—were there any lessons given to the children?"

"Oh, yes," Berthe assured her. "But the children won't pay heed. They run away and hide. Mademoiselle Justine bit Fräulein Schloss, and the baron slapped her for it. Soon after that the fräulein went away and there have been no governesses since."

The situation was becoming clearer. At eighteen, Anne might have no practical experience of life, but she had not read the poems of Lord Byron or the novels of Mrs. Radclyffe without becoming aware of the less savoury aspects of life.

The frail wife, the demanding husband, the procession of young women, the defiant children. From somewhere deep within herself there rose a cold, fierce anger. She had no idea why it should affect her so personally, but she knew beyond any shadow of doubt that she must do everything she could to set matters right.

"We had better begin to sort the linen," she said, rising. "Most of it will need bleaching in the sun. The counterpanes and curtains will require mending too. Some of them are sadly torn. I cannot possibly do it entirely alone."

"There are two seamstresses in the village," Berthe told her. "They'd be glad of the money."

"And we will require extra women for the cleaning. It will take at least a month." Anne stopped, biting her lip. "I must speak to the baron. Do you know where he's likely to be at this hour?"

"He generally rides out," Berthe began, then interrupted herself as she glaned towards the window. "No, he's just now coming up the steps."

"Begin to collect the linen." Anne marched towards the door, two determined spots of colour burning in her cheeks. "I intend to speak to the baron."

The baron, it became clear, also wished to speak to her. His voice echoed along the corridor.

"Mademoiselle Sayle! Here!"

"Sir, I wish to have a few words." Anne, hurrying into the main hall almost bumped into him.

"Mademoiselle, what the devil do you think you're doing?" He took a step back and glowered down at her.

"Doing?" Anne stared up at him, noticing with trepidation, the clenched jaw and twitching nerve over his temple.

"Doing!" He repeated loudly. "I cannot find anyone to saddle my horse or obey any command I intend to give. Instead, I find my kitchens awash with buckets of soapy water, with bins of evil smelling refuse, with piles of tangled linen—and I am informed it is being done by my orders, relayed by the English mademoiselle! You have not been four-and-twenty hours under my roof, and you are turning the entire household on its head!"

"You told me to make myself useful," Anne said, recovering her voice. "I have decided that the chateau would benefit from an entire cleaning, and as I could not do it alone—"

"You issued orders in my name to my servants!"

"They did not seem overburdened with work," Anne said dryly. "I will begin the mending of the linen tomorrow, but it will be necessary to engage extra servants for a few weeks. That was what I wished to speak to you about."

"Oh, I cannot imagine why you troubled," he said.

"Why not engage them without bothering to consult me?"

"Because they will require payment, sir, and I cannot guarantee them payment until I have your word," she explained.

"Oh, I will pay them," he said. "Pray don't imagine that I am without the necessary funds."

"I am not in the habit of imagining," Anne said, not altogether truthfully.

"But you are in the habit of taking matters into your own hands. I do wonder how the estimable Miss Turnbull is contriving to manage her school now that you have left."

"I merely made myself useful there," Anne said.

"I have the most uncomfortable sensation that when you begin to make yourself useful, everybody in your neighbourhood must prepare for an exhausting time," the baron said. The twitching nerve had stilled and he had relaxed his jaw muscles.

"If you disapprove—"

"No, no." He waved a hand about the immense hall. "If you can bring some order out of this—chaos, you have my leave. My wife was bred to aristocratic habits and cannot be brought to any recognition of her duty. She spent her childhood in the south, where the events of the Revolution scarcely touched her. She had no experience of being the chatelaine of a large house when I married her, and she has not cared to learn since."

"I will do what I regard as necessary, sir, subject to your and the baroness's approval," Anne said. A shade of coldness had crept into her voice. It was not only ill-bred but unkind of Jean Lanuit to talk so contemptuously of his wife to anyone, let alone an employee.

"How disapproving and English you sound," he said, lazily mocking. "Very well. Make whatever arrangements you deem necessary, and I will pay—eventually."

He gave her a little bow and strode out, leaving her gazing after him with a troubled expression on her face.

It was small wonder that the children behaved so abominably when their mother remained in her rooms and their father obviously made a point of seducing the governesses. It was an appalling situation, one about which she had surreptitiously read, but never expected to encounter. She wondered why the baroness should regard a sewing maid as immune to her husband's advances.

Perhaps the baron himself considered a governess, being higher in the social scale, as more worthy of his attentions. Certainly he was not attracted to herself. She was too plain to arouse desire and too independent to awaken compassion. It was as well that she was not in the least attracted to Jean Lanuit, she told herself, and went back to Berthe who had started to pile up sheets, blankets, bolster cases, tablecloths, and towels in a heap that made Anne glad two seamstresses were coming to lend a hand.

It was late afternoon before she had finished the sorting of the linen. Some of it was too worn and discoloured to be of any use save as dishrags and dusters, much of the rest needed darning, and it was all slightly grubby. Yet the linen was finely woven, the silk shot with gold and silver thread, the blankets of thick fleecy wool.

Berthe had departed briefly and returned with a tray on which a chicken salad and a bowl of compote were set. The dishes were still slightly damp from a recent immersion in hot water, and the tray had been scrubbed free of rust. Someone had clearly gone to some trouble to please the extraordinary newcomer who was bent on changing everything. Anne ate and instructed Berthe to compliment the cook.

"Monsieur Louis is telling everybody it is time that this household was properly arranged," the girl said. "He is most pleased to think that soon he will have a clean kitchen to rule over."

"Has it been—has the baroness been sick for a long time?" Anne asked.

"Since Mademoiselle Justine was born, I believe. That was two years before I came, Mademoiselle."

"You are from Paris?"

"*Oui.* I am an orphan, and so this was a good situation for me to find. You have a family?"

"Only an—no family. I, too, am an orphan."

It had been on the tip of her tongue to mention her uncle. She must not allow her enthusiasm for the task she had undertaken to cause her to relax her vigilance.

"It is very sad to be an orphan, *n'est ce pas?*" Berthe said cheerfully, poking her finger through a hole in a sheet and examining her nail.

"Yes. Yes. I suppose it is."

Anne paused to consider. She could not, of course, remember her mother at all, for that lady had died at her birth. But her childhood had been happy. She recalled her father's laughter, the ladies and gentlemen who thronged to the ivied manor house, the sound of the horn as the pink coated huntsmen had streamed across the meadow.

It was odd that, though she had often tried, she could never recall her father whole and entire. She could only recapture a fleeting, brilliant glimpse of some part of him—his laugh, his arms tossing her in the air, his legs encased in shiny black boots descending a staircase. Yet she had been ten when he had been thrown from his horse and died instantly of a broken neck.

"I think this completes the linen." She rose, dusting down her dress. "Do you know where the baron is?"

"He has ridden out," Berthe said. "He'll likely be away for two or three days. He often stays in town."

It was a pity, Anne thought, that he had not confined his amours to town instead of bringing them beneath his roof.

"I think I will take supper in the room next to my bedchamber," she decided. The room, which she had marked on her tour of inspection, was furnished as a sitting room and had been marginally less grubby than most of the others.

"You will not be eating with us?" Berthe looked surprised.

Another error! Obviously sewing maids were expected to sit down with all the other servants, not eat in solitary state.

"In England," she invented rapidly, "the woman who sews for the household has her own room where she takes her meals."

"I can light a fire and bring up a tray," Berthe said, accepting the explanation.

Anne went up to her bedchamber, feeling weary, but pleasantly so. If she could achieve some kind of order in the running of the household before she handed in her notice and returned to England, she would feel satisfied. It would also be pleasant if she could coax some response from the two children. They were not her concern, but her heart had been moved by their neglected condition. The baron could not

56

wholly be blamed for it. Even though the baroness was sick, she ought to have made some arrangements for the care of the children.

She had found some pink brocade rolled up in the middle of a pile of towels. It would make a very pretty dress for a small girl with dark curly hair. Anne had taken it with her and had spread it out on the bed when the door opened and the curly head she had been thinking about was poked in, the rest of Justine following as her brother pushed her in the back.

"You have not been near us all day," Gaston accused.

"I am not employed to look after you," Anne said, "only to sew your clothes and do what seems necessary in the house."

"Everywhere is being washed, except mama's chambers—and papa's of course, but his are clean already," the boy said.

They would be, Anne thought, compressing her lips. The rest of them could live in squalour, but Jean Lanuit was the kind of man who would insist on his own quarters being maintained in fastidious order.

"What's that?" Justine had approached and was pointing at the brocade.

"A new dress for you when I have cut it out and found needles and thread—if you want it," Anne said carefully.

"She has dresses," Gaston began haughtily, but Justine interrupted him shrilly.

"I do want it! I do!"

"Why? Nobody ever comes," he argued.

"Now that your father has given orders for the chateau to be cleaned, perhaps there will be guests," Anne said. "You will not wish to appear before guests looking as you do now."

"We have to go." Gaston seized his sister's hand. "We have our supper with maman when she is felling strong enough."

"Good evening then." Anne smiled and began to roll up the brocade.

At the door Gaston paused and said, with the air of one making a great concession, "If you wish you may make me a new tunic and breeches, after Justine's dress is finished."

— 3 —

THE BARON STAYED away for more than a week and, as the baroness never put her nose outside her apartments, the spring cleaning of the chateau continued without interruption. The upper floors in the west wing were the family apartments, where Anne did not presume to venture, but on the ground floor were several large sitting rooms which, when scrubbed and polished, revealed themselves as apartments of charm and distinction. The kitchen and adjoining pantries were now so spotless that Monsieur Louis declared proudly it was possible to eat off the floor, and, in a long room originally designated as a store room, two apple-cheeked seamstresses worked industriously filling the surrounding shelves with washed and mended linen.

Gaston and Justine, having tired of their game of indifference, spent a considerable time exploring the newly shining premises. They also came to be fitted for their new garments, though Gaston changed his mind about the breeches, saying he was too old to have a woman make them. He did, however, condescend to let Anne fit him for an overtunic, which she planned to make out of a length of white satin. He had even gone to the trouble of washing his hands and face and tugging a comb through his wild, dark hair. Anne wisely made no comment on it, but patiently measured him while Justine gazed with wide, dark eyes at the simple gown that had been fashioned from the pink brocade.

"Is it for a party?" she enquired. "Are we going to have a party?"

"Don't be foolish!" Her brother scowled at her. "We don't have parties."

"Perhaps you will begin to have them," Anne said, "when your father returns from Paris."

Gaston gave her a frowning look. "And then you will put on a beautiful dress and turn into a governess."

"I do not intend to turn into anything," Anne said calmly. "I am the sewing maid and nothing more. Who gives you your lessons now, anyway?"

"We read with maman when she is not too tired, and sometimes the curé comes," Gaston told her.

It sounded like a most unsatisfactory education, but, as it was none of her business, she held her tongue. If the baron and his wife were content to see their children growing up wild and undisciplined, there was nothing she could do about it, but the temptation to try was growing stronger. At least they were beginning to speak English when she addressed them, and though they didn't go so far as to thank her, she sensed they were both pleased with the new clothes.

Berthe had attached herself to Anne as firmly as a stray puppy, happily trotting on the errands Anne required, bringing her meals up from the kitchen. She was a loyal little soul who was not content unless someone was giving instructions. Indeed, Anne gained the distinct impression that all the servants responded well to the fever of activity that had swept the neglected household.

She was on her knees in the room she had appropriated as a sitting room, cutting out the sleeves for Gaston's tunic, when Berthe came to inform her she had a visitor.

"Doctor de Reynard, Mademoiselle." Berthe hesitated, then added, "He is very handsome, I think."

"He's a—a friend." Rising to her feet, Anne felt an unaccountable embarrassment. At least she supposed it was embarrassment that coloured her cheeks as she went down the stairs.

The great entrance hall was empty. Feeling a little puzzled, Anne walked out to the terrace and spotted the young doctor at the far end of it near a side door. Clearly he had gone to what he assumed to be the servants' entrance.

He turned as she approached, and she was struck with pleasure at the sight of his cordial smile and well-knit frame, the fair hair that clustered thickly over his well-shaped head.

"Miss Sayle, I am happy to see you well settled," he said, taking her hand. "I took the liberty of calling in the hope that you might be permitted some time off in order to take a drive with me." There was a pony trap on the path below the steps, and he nodded towards it invitingly.

"How did you know where to find me?" she asked.

"I have the power of mind reading," he said gravely. "Also the address was written on your luggage labels."

She laughed, amused at her own stupidity. "I would enjoy a drive, provided it lasts no longer than an hour. Would you wait while I get my pelisse and bonnet?"

"Of course." He began to walk down the steps toward the pony trap.

Her pelisse and high crowned bonnet—or rather Anna's—were of the same light grey as her dress and very plainly cut, but the bonnet had dark red ribbons and a feathery plume of dark red, and a hasty glance in the mirror just before she went downstairs did not displease her. There was a lively sparkle in her eyes, and her cheeks were pink.

"Are you going somewhere, Mademoiselle?" Berthe asked, as Anne passed her in the corridor.

"For a drive with my friend. I'll return in an hour."

She went with a light step down the stairs, aware that this was the first time in her life she had been invited to drive out with a man and pleased that it was the attractive young doctor.

"You look as if your situation agreed with you," he complimented her as he helped her to her seat.

"It is much more interesting than I imagined it would be," she agreed. "There is a lot of sewing to be done, but I have two women to help me, then the chateau is being cleaned and refurbished, and so the entire household is fully occupied all day long."

They were trotting through the open gates, and he glanced at her as he guided the pony into the road. "You have met your employers?"

"The Baroness Sophie is an invalid who keeps mainly to her chambers, but, naturally, I met her. The children, too—Gaston is nine, and Justine is six."

"And the baron?" He had his eyes on the road ahead and was not looking at her.

"Baron Lanuit was there when I arrived, but he has been away this past week."

"He has an unfortunate reputation," Edouard de Reynard said. "In Paris, he is spoken of as a rake and a libertine."

"You have heard the baron discussed in Paris?" Anne said, surprised.

"I took it upon myself to make enquiry," he answered.

"Took it upon yourself!" she echoed indignantly. "What gave you the right to take it upon yourself?"

"Nothing and nobody, but I wished to ascertain if the people for whom you were going to work would be likely to treat you with the courtesy and consideration you deserve," he said.

It was a disarming answer, but she was not completely disarmed. It had been a violation of her independence on his part, which brought home to her again the difficulties of being a lone female.

"Miss Turnbull, my former employer, had a highly developed sense of responsibility," she said coldly. "You cannot imagine she did not make her own enquiries."

"I am certain she did." He had flushed slightly. "I had no right to make such enquiries, but our time together on the boat was so agreeable that I felt as if we were already friends of long-standing. I was informed when I mentioned the name of Lanuit to my late uncle's lawyer that Jean Lanuit spends most of his time in gambling and wenching while his estate goes to ruin through neglect. I was hesitant at first, but then I decided no harm could come from my driving out to see you and finding if all was as it should be."

"How very gallant of you," Anne said tartly, "and what, pray, did you intend to do if you found that everything was not as it should be?"

"I hoped to offer you the means to return to England. It was, as you rightly charge, unwarranted interference on my part, but kindly meant."

"Then I shall accept it as such." Relenting, she awarded him a faint smile. "However, as you can see your fears were groundless. I am satisfied with the position. Indeed I am treated more as a housekeeper than a sewing maid."

"And the baron?"

"A good servant does not discuss her employers. The baron's habits are not my concern provided he pays my salary regularly. Oh! but this is charming!"

The cry broke from her as they left the main road and entered a park gay with flowers. Broad avenues of trees stretched beyond the neatly trimmed lawns and flowerbeds.

"I noticed it from the road as I was driving to Paris," Edouard de Reynard said. "Apparently it is part of a large estate, but this park is open to the public."

"And for children too." As the pony trap slowed down, Anne nodded towards a railed space within which were swings, seesaws, and a brightly painted roundabout on which several children clung to hobby horses while a tinkling sound shivered on the breeze. Their mothers and nurses sat on benches in the shade of the trees, exchanging gossip and knitting, and one little girl bowled a hoop up and down one of the paths.

"Shall we stroll for a few minutes?" He hitched the pony to a rail and assisted her to alight.

They walked slowly, enjoying the sunlight that made dancing leaf patterns on the ground and the warm breeze that carried with it all the scents of the blossoms. Her fingertips lightly on her escort's arm, Anne was conscious of latent vitality and strength in the muscles beneath the broadcloth of his coat. Though he was above average height, he was not powerfully built—steel rather than iron, she considered, but steel had resilience and strength.

"To whom does the estate belong?" she asked.

"I have no idea. I passed it on the way to the Château Lanuit and marked it as a spot where we might break off our ride," he said.

"It is certainly delightful." Anne looked about her

with pleasure as they left the main avenue and strolled down one of the leafy paths that twisted to the lawn before the high walls that obviously divided the private part of the estate from that open to the public. In front of them a mermaid carved from green stone sat on the rim of a small fountain, and water cascaded from the open mouths of fishes clustered around her.

"There is an inscription!" Anne went forward eagerly to look, but the silver plaque bore only a name. " 'Toinette du Bois," she read. "I wonder who she is, or was."

"Probably a relative of whoever owns the park." Her companion was not looking at the fountain but at Anne, and his eyes were frankly admiring.

She became aware of his regard and felt the colour rise in her face again. She was also conscious of the fact that they stood in a relatively isolated spot, shielded by a high hedge from the children on the roundabout.

"How did your business go in Paris?" She began to speak rapidly, a pulse beating in her throat. "You have been with the lawyer, you said?"

"Dealing with my inheritance." He made a wry face. "The house was damaged during the Revolution and has been neglected since. I have arranged for some repairs and redecoration to be carried out while I am here, and then I shall sell it."

"How long are—how long will that take?" She ran her fingers over the serrated green stone of the mermaid's tail.

"About two months."

"And then you will hang out your shingle in Quebec? You are not impressed by the Old World?"

"Tremendously impressed—as a visitor. I am in the middle of a history book with all the pages being rapidly turned. One grows dizzy with cathedrals, palaces, sites of famous happenings. But I was reared in a different place." He hesitated, clearly trying to marshal his thoughts. "In Québec, there are the old traditions, too, kept up by people like my parents, but there are also wider horizons. There is space for the new to enter and change and carry everything forward. There are forests of ancient trees so thick it would take a dozen men to circle them round and lakes that are frozen solid in the winter so that one may sledge for many miles upon them, and tribes—Indian tribes—who have still scarcely seen a white man. It is a crude, raw country in many ways, but it offers a challenge and a promise."

"It is a place for an ambitious man," Anne said, "and you are ambitious, Doctor de Reynard."

"I wish to help shape the future," he said and, looking at her, smiled. "That must sound like one of the most arrogant statements ever made, but there it must stand."

"I remember Miss Turnbull telling us once that a little arrogance in the young is excusable."

"Us?" He gave her a slightly puzzled look.

"The pupils and servants always attended morning assembly," Anne said quickly. "She generally gave a short talk on some moral or ethical issue. One could not avoid listening."

"You, at least, appear to have listened to some purpose."

"Oh, sewing is not an occupation that uses up all one's mental capacities," she said and seeing his expression remained puzzled, went on, "My father was something of a scholar, I believe, so I may have inherited some bent for learning from him."

"I thought you mentioned during our conversation on the boat that you were reared in an orphange."

"Certain enquiries were made, I believe," she said vaguely, and began to saunter back towards the playground.

It was becoming extraordinarily difficult for her to remember the part she had decided to play. The trouble was that the real Anna had never been the typical maidservant either, having been given the benefit by Miss Turnbull of some education. It was harder to assume the role of a half-educated girl than that of an illiterate.

"I have offended you in some way?" Edouard de Reynard caught up with her. "I fear you regard my interest in you as an impertinence?"

"No, of course not! It is merely that I am not accustomed to talking so much about myself," she said quickly. "I find myself a very dull subject, to tell you the truth. I would greatly prefer to hear more about your work. Did you always wish to be a physician and heal the sick?"

"When I was very small, I longed to be a fur trapper," he said laughing. "The mountain men used to come down into Québec to barter their skins, and they seemed to me to be taller than any other men in the world. Very fierce with their shaggy beards and loud voices and the big knives stuck in their belts."

"So you became a physician in order to cut people up," she teased.

"Oh, I think I became interested in anatomy. I wanted to find out what makes people work, and why some organs became diseased, and how one could put them right. And how of two people suffering from the same illness, one will recover and the other will die."

She listened, glancing occasionally at his happy, animated expression and feeling the stirrings of envy because he knew who he was and what he wanted out of life. He was not hampered by conventions, nor forced to snatch a scant couple of months in which to carry out a project close to his heart.

They had reached the pony trap. "Hired for the afternoon," her companion interrupted himself to say. "I hoped that we might spend more time together, but I am grateful for even this brief interlude. You have the disposal of your own time to a very large extent, it appears?"

"It seems that I do. The household is—" Anne hesitated, not wishing to appear a gossip. "The household is run on somewhat disorganized lines."

"Which you intend to set right?"

"Heavens, how domineering that makes me sound!" She accepted his hand up to her seat. "There is a vast quantity of sewing to be done, and I have been bidden to make myself generally useful. I assure you there is no more to it than that."

"And the baroness is sick?"

"She had been invalid since Justine—that is her daughter who is six—was born. She is still a young woman and would be beautiful were she in better health, but, as to what precisely is wrong, I have no idea."

"Probably her physicians are not certain either." Taking up the reins, he flicked them lightly across the pony's back. "Some wealthy women take refuge from boredom or unhappiness in illness. They think themselves sick and so become so."

"That's a little harsh!" She protested.

"Not at all, they don't do so deliberately. I am of the opinion that when a healthy person believes herself to be sick she is actually suffering from something that cannot be diagnosed from any study of anatomy. And then, of course, the poor lady may be suffering from some chronic ailment of which we have no knowledge. Do you have much to do with the children?"

"Not very much. They are—somewhat shy with foreigners."

"I am sure that, with your charm, you will quickly make them your friends. I hope you will have the leisure and inclination to come out with me again. I would like to show you Paris."

"But I don't have a—" Anne bit off the word 'chaperone' as she remembered in time that sewing maids were not expected to have them and ended somewhat lamely, "suitable clothes to wear."

"What you have on now is perfectly suitable for some sightseeing and a light meal somewhere," he replied. "Shall we say in five days' time? I will call for you at ten in the morning and return you to the chateau before evening. Your employer cannot object to that."

"No. No, I suppose not."

"Perhaps you yourself do not wish to come?" He looked suddenly boyishly ill at ease. "I am aware that I have, from the beginning, thrust my company on you somewhat unceremoniously."

"I would like to come very much," she said firmly, thrusting aside her own doubts as coy and missish. The young man had offered nothing but a friendly invitation at which no sensible, independent girl would balk. It was romantic foolishness to make any more of it especially when, in a couple of months, he would be returning to Québec to set up his medical practice.

They were bowling along the highway. The park, she realised, was no farther than a brisk walk from the chateau. It might be agreeable to stroll there herself one day and enjoy an hour's complete privacy. She could take pad and pencil and plan the final form her book would take. Although she had been several days in France, her duties had left her so weary that at the end of the day she had fallen straight into bed and not even begun to sort out her notes. From now on she must make more efficient use of her time.

"You can leave me at the gates," Anne said as they hove into view. "I can walk up to the chateau."

"When I call for a girl," he said firmly, "I always deliver her back to the same place."

So he had taken other girls for drives. It was natural that he had, for he was in his midtwenties and, though studying would have precluded his entering into matrimony, he would certainly have known young women, flirted with them, perhaps fallen in love. She had no way of knowing and not the smallest right to enquire.

"You have not changed your mind about spending a few hours in Paris with me?" He gave her a slightly anxious glance as they reached the bottom of the steps, and he drew the pony to a halt.

"I am looking forward to it." Allowing him to help her down, she was aware of the warm strength of his clasp, of his blue eyes smiling steadily down into hers.

"I too," he said, "look forward to it. I enjoy your company very much, Miss Sayle."

It was relief and disappointment when he released his clasp and climbed up to the driving seat again. For all his youth, he exuded a sense of purpose and determination that matched her own. Raising her hand in farewell and climbing the steps she found herself wondering how it would feel to be kissed by him.

Two figures headed towards her from the end of the terrace. Gaston, clutching Justine by the hand as usual, skidded to a stop on the paved flagstones and said accusingly, "You went out with a man without telling us!"

"With a friend, and why should I tell you?" she enquired.

"Is he your lover?" Gaston asked.

The child could not possibly know what he was saying, but the word, spoken in French with its overtones of voluptuous langour, made her cheeks burn.

"He is a physician," she began.

"Are you sick, Mademoiselle? Are you going to be sick and die slowly like maman?" Justine demanded, her dark eyes wide in her pale face.

"Of course I am not sick, and your mama is not going to die for a very long time!" Anne wondered who could have put such a notion into the little girl's head. "Doctor de Reynard is a friend of mine."

"The other governesses did not have gentlemen friends," Gaston remarked.

"I have told you before that I am not a governess," Anne said patiently, "and I have one gentleman friend."

"Maman wishes to see you." Gaston's voice broke into her last word.

"Now?"

"Before you take off your hat," Justine said, obviously quoting.

"Then I will come at once."

With a slight sinking of the heart, Anne went with the children along the terrace and through the side door. She supposed that she ought to have asked leave before driving away with Edouard de Reynard. In many houses the servants were not allowed followers. Again she had completely forgotten the station in society she was now supposed to occupy.

The children ran ahead of her when they reached

the staircase leading to the private apartments in the west wing and had already tapped on the door of their mother's chamber and been admitted when Anne arrived on the threshold.

As upon the previous occasion, the overcrowded room was in gloom, but, as she entered, Gaston, at a murmured command of his mother's, opened one of the shutters to admit more light.

"You may leave me," the baroness said, and the two of them, instantly obedient, went out, Gaston holding his sister's hand.

"Such a responsibility," the baroness said, her eyes following them.

"They are fine children, Madame." Anne said and instantly despised herself for sounding servile.

"You have been out?" The baroness leaned back against her pillows. She was wearing a robe of dusky pink wool above which her face, framed by its crown of heavy chestnut hair, was startlingly white.

"I realise I ought to have asked permission," Anne began.

"On the contrary, you are entitled to take time from your work," the baroness interrupted. "We were not aware you had friends here in Paris."

"Doctor de Reynard and I met on the boat coming over, Madame," Anne explained. "He is from Québec but has business in Paris this summer."

"A physician?" There was a slight quickening of interest in the languid voice.

"Yes, Madame. He is newly qualified but seems most dedicated."

"And he has a *tendresse* for you?"

Anne was about to disclaim it, but some nuance in the other's tone made her pause. The baroness had an eager, hopeful expression on her face. What was it

Gaston had said? "The other governesses did not have gentlemen friends."

"I believe the doctor does—admire me," she admitted.

"And we are most happy that you have such a friend, Mademoiselle!" There was no mistaking the relief in the voice.

"He has invited me to spend some hours with him sightseeing in Paris."

"Then you must certainly go. Your work here has already, I am told, made a difference. The children tell me everything is being made as grand as if we were to hold a ball."

"You may see for yourself if you choose, Madame," Anne said eagerly. "I hope that I have not exceeded my duties, but it would have been foolish to wash and mend all the linen and replace it in rooms that were dir—less than clean."

"You need not trouble to spare my feelings," the baroness said. "If I were not such a sad invalid, I would supervise the household arrangements more thoroughly, but the truth is that I never really could even before the children were born. In the south, where I was born, the climate is warmer and drier and the people more carefree than here in the north. Here everybody talks still of the Terror and the wars under the Emperor as if it all might happen again, and one is expected to oversee everything oneself. Oh, we have engaged housekeepers and valets, but I fear they have all turned out badly. My health is simply not equal to the responsibility." She sounded petulant, like a small girl who has not yet grown up.

Anne controlled a spurt of irritation and spoke gently. "I believe, Madame, that if you were to find the strength to visit the other apartments in the chateau, you would give the servants pleasure and encourage them to work harder. Once everything is in order, I believe you would have no difficulty in finding a responsible elderly person to manage the household."

"If my health were better—" the baroness murmured, and then sighed. "One cannot ask for miracles! Enquire of your friend if he has any knowledge of new treatments."

"For what ailment, Madame?" Anne enquired bluntly.

"For general weakness, attacks of giddiness and nausea, headaches that pound my skull."

"I will ask him, Madame, but surely your own physicians—"

"They know nothing. Nothing! They suggest one treatment after another, but none of them work."

"I will ask him," Anne said, bobbing a curtsey as the white hand waved her away. She thought she heard the baroness demanding that the shutters be closed again as she went down the stairs, but she ignored the voice. The baroness, however ill she might genuinely be, half-enjoyed her indisposition, and, as she was not helpless, it would not kill her to draw the shutter herself.

The children had run off somewhere, but Berthe tagged along behind her as she went into the east wing.

"Did you have a good time, Mademoiselle? Your friend is most handsome, is he not? Is he a Frenchman?"

"French-Canadian, I suppose."

"And he has followed you here because he is mad for love of you and cannot live without you."

"He has business in Paris and merely came here to see if I had settled in well," Anne said laughing, "so you may leave your romantic notions in your pocket!"

"The English are so cold," Berthe said sadly. "But he did take you for a drive."

"To a very pretty park quite near here." Anne was taking off her bonnet as she entered her room.

"With wooden horses for the children to ride?"

"Do you know who owns it?" Anne enquired.

"A mad countess." Berthe rolled her small eyes.

"A mad—! Berthe, don't be so foolish!"

"It is the truth, Mademoiselle," the girl insisted. "The Countess du Bois is known to be mad. She lives in a chateau beyond the park and wears still the garments of the *ancien régime*, with a wig upon her head and her skirts hooped. She never leaves the chateau—"

"Then how do you know all this?"

"The gardener is a friend of mine," Berthe said, clasping her hands together and fluttering her meagre eyelashes. "He sees her when she walks in her gardens. Gabrielle du Bois, she is named."

"Not 'Toinette?"

"Ah, you saw the fountain!" Berthe nodded, pleased to be imparting information. " 'Toinette was her daughter, Mademoiselle. She was guillotined during the Terror. The park was opened in her memory."

"So that living children could have pleasure." Anne smiled. "Perhaps the countess is not mad in an unpleasant way at all."

"I do not believe she is dangerous," Berthe said, "but mad is mad. Me, I stay away! Does Mademoiselle wish for supper yet?"

"I'll finish the tunic for Gaston first. In a couple of hours, I'd like something if you can bring it."

"I am glad to bring whatever you want," Berthe said simply.

"It is very good of you to help me in the way you

do," Anne said on impulse as the other went towards the door. "I hope it does not inconvenience you to fetch and carry for another servant."

"I don't think of you as a servant," Berthe said, half-turning. "I think you are a—a princess in disguise, and one day you will put on your jewels and tell us why you have been hiding."

"I am certainly not a princess!" Anne said sharply. "Why, I never heard such nonsense. It is merely that I am English, and you have probably never met many English people before—and, if I had any jewels, I should not be earning my living mending linen, I promise you."

"You don't act like a servant," Berthe said obstinately as she went out.

She had unwittingly stumbled on the weakness in Anne's ability to play Anna's role. It was not impossible to deceive the aristocracy into regarding one as a servant, since many people never even troubled to look at their domestics, but a real servant would sense the presence of an impostor.

Anne sighed as she picked up the scissors and bent over the white satin. The truth was that, since arriving in France, she had been suspended between two worlds, and she was no longer certain in which one she wished to be.

=== 4 ===

"I WAS AFRAID that you might change your mind and decide not to come." Edouard de Reynard glanced at her as they drove towards Paris. He had arrived punctually in the hired trap, and she had felt a genuine delight at seeing him again.

"I do not usually break promises," she reproached him.

"And I hope this was one you did not wish to break?"

"I have looked forward to it," she said, "not merely because it is an outing for me but also because I will have your company."

"Miss Sayle, you are a remarkable young woman!" he exclaimed.

"Because I enjoy your company?"

"Because you tell me so frankly without false coyness or maidenly flutterings."

"With which you, as a physician, have small patience?"

"Which I find amusing, but irritating, when one wishes for an open and honest relationship."

Anne smiled but a little of her pleasure at being with him was dulled. There could be no prospect of genuine honesty between them while she was still playing a part and, by the time she gave in her notice and returned to England, he would be on the high seas bound for Canada. He would be embarking on a satisfying career, whereas she would be meeting an uncle who would be furiously angry at the deception she had practised.

To divert her mind from the somewhat gloomy track it was following she said brightly, "This is my first visit to a foreign city. I hope that you will be able to point out the places of interest to me."

"Since my arrival I seem to have spent much of my time closeted with lawyers, estate agents, and architects," he said ruefully, "but I have continued to find my way around. We are coming now towards the Champs-Élysées. All the fashionable people drive up here. We will stable the pony and take our meal in a restaurant near the Louvre. Then we can stroll on foot if the weather continues warm."

They had entered the outskirts of the city, and Anne's problems were temporarily pushed to the back of her mind as she gazed about her with lively interest. The narrow cobbled streets were opening out into a broad avenue lined with handsome buildings, with here and there an open green space. The avenue was crowded with gigs and carriages, their equipage sparkling, footmen standing tall and straight at the back. There were also many people walking, the ladies balancing huge beribboned bonnets above narrow skirted, ruched dresses, their escorts top-hatted, their coats cut away to display frilled shirts and dark, embroidered waist-coats.

"The Palace of the Tuileries is not far," Edouard de Reyndard informed her. "The royal family tried to escape from there but were found and brought back. The Swiss guards were butchered in the courtyard and the royal apartments looted. That must have been a terrible day."

"One would not imagine now that such things had ever occurred," Anne marvelled, looking at the elegant crowds.

"The Emperor Napoleon made it his official residence. Now most of it is given over to the Civil Service as offices, but it is possible to pay a fee and see a few of the State Apartments. There are restaurants nearby, so we can eat first. The one we are going to was recommended by my uncle's lawyer as a place where one can eat well, so, if we do not enjoy the meal, we can lay the blame upon him!"

He drew up and, alighting, assisted her to do so. Again she was conscious of his firm grasp, of the admiration in his blue eyes. It puzzled her, for she was well aware of the deficiencies in her own appearance. Though she knew she was looking her best, she also knew that she could not begin to compete with the many pretty young ladies to be seen in the most fashionable of cities.

He had left her side for a few minutes to see to the stabling of the pony, and now he returned, offering his arm. "That is the Pavillon de Flore and that the Pavillon de Marsan." He indicated the huge buildings ahead of them. "The palace between them is the Tuileries, and the Louvre lies beyond."

"Will some of the paintings of David be in the museum?" she enquired.

"You have heard of the artist David?' He looked at her in surprise.

"Miss Turnbull had some reproductions at the school," she said hurriedly. "Naturally, when one dusts something one becomes interested in it. Is this the restaurant your uncle's lawyer recommended?"

"Now we will test his opinion." He smiled at her as they entered the panelled interior with its air of faded gentility. Certainly, it looked the kind of respectable place to which one might safely bring a maiden aunt.

Half an hour later, eating the *mousseline de saumon* that had followed the onion soup and *gougères* stuffed with mushrooms, she smiled across the table at her companion, saying, "Your uncle's lawyer knows how to choose fine food. I hope he is as expert at his profession."

"Efficient at everything I would say. Fortunately there are no complications over the inheritance. The house is mine to dispose of as I think fit."

"And you will sell."

"As I told you before, the Old World has a great interest and fascination for me, but I am rooted in the New and will build my future there. Paris can only be an interlude."

He was probably including her in the "interlude." She kept the bright smile on her face, inwardly scolding herself for the disappointment that flooded her. It was utterly stupid to allow herself to feel this way about the first young man with whom she had ever had anything that approached a friendship. And she had been the one who had drawn back from the idea of being paraded on the marriage market!

"I beg your pardon?" He had asked some question to which she had not been paying attention.

"I asked if you had made any plans yourself."

"Plans? Well, I am employed by the Lanuit family—"

"As their sewing maid. With your intelligence I am sure you could obtain a much better situation as governess or something of that nature."

"Oh, I have picked up bits and pieces of knowledge," she said lightly, "and Miss Turnbull never treated me precisely as a domestic, but I am not qualified to teach children. I am not even sure I would wish to do so. As it is, my position at Chateau Lanuit gives me a certain degree of privacy and some leisure time. For the moment I am satisfied."

"You strike me as a young lady with ambition," he persisted.

"Oh, we all have ambitions, I suppose." She still spoke lightly, wishing she could tell him about the carefully collected notes, the story that was rounded and perfect in her head, needing only to be set down on paper to become a reality. But sewing maids, even if they had received some education, did not aspire to be novelists. Indeed, apart from one or two exceptions like Mrs. Edgeworth, most females, whatever their station, did not aspire to write for publication at all.

The waiter was serving almond cake, thick with whipped cream, and coffee in tiny gold-rimmed cups. Taking up her fork, she concentrated on the meal, determined to enjoy every mouthful. If this was only an interlude, then she would be foolish not to derive as much pleasure as possible from the occasion.

"Even Monsieur Louis does not cook like this," she commented.

"Monsieur Louis?"

"The cook at the chateau. He has become a friend" She had not intended to gossip but soon found herself telling her companion about the spring cleaning that had begun at the chateau.

"The serv—the other servants were very enthusiastic once the work was begun. And yesterday an army of gardeners arrived to cut the lawns and trim the hedges. The baroness will be astonished if she ever leaves her apartments to see the difference that has been wrought already."

"Is she so much of an invalid?"

"It's difficult to tell." Anne frowned slightly. "She certainly appears to be very frail and delicate, and her face is as white as paper. She was very interested when I told her my friend was a physician and enquired if you had new treatment for her ailment, but she was very vague as to what that ailment was. She has headaches and giddiness, she told me, but I did wonder if she were not using them as an excuse because she cannot run her household properly. I think she wishes to be well, and, yet, she also enjoys being sick."

"And the baron?"

"He is expected home tonight, I believe. I suppose his business is concluded. I don't know what he feels about his wife's illness. I am not in his confidence."

"I suspect his behaviour may have something to do with his wife's sickness," Edouard de Reynard said thoughtfully, "but it is unprofessional of me even to hazard an opinion, since I have not been called in to diagnose or suggest treatment."

"Would you, if the baroness asked for you?"

"I am qualified, but I am not certain how the law stands here and whether, as a visitor, I would be permitted to practise—and I am not seeking out patients anyway."

His smile robbed the words of their curtness. Rising, he summoned the waiter to ask for the bill, and Anne thought how splendid it would be if he could be persuaded to treat the baroness. Then, when Anne herself returned to England, she would leave behind her a happy and orderly household. She had no idea why she should regard such a task as her own responsibility, but something inside her had felt an immense relief when she saw the windows of the chateau sparkling and the two children with their faces washed and their wild black hair tamed.

They left the restaurant and strolled towards the palace. Close to, it was overwhelming. She felt as small as an ant as they went through the gates into the courtyard. Here were the stones on which the Swiss guards, fighting to defend the royal family from the mob, had shed their blood. Within were the rooms where men like Robespierre and Marat had sat in judgement on people who, for no crime save that of being well-born, were sent immediately to the guillotine. Anne wondered if the daughter of the mad countess had been among those sentenced here and, if so, how the mother had managed to survive.

The apartments had been occupied later by the Empress Josephine and glittered still with crystal chandeliers and brocaded curtains and Sévres ornaments, but the former tragedies of the place still lingered like a pall over the splendour and luxury.

When they emerged she said impulsively, "How I should hate to live in such a place with so many sad and violent memories!"

"My sentiments exactly!" Edouard de Reynard looked pleased as he always did whenever she made some remark that coincided with his own opinion. "The past presses in all around. In Canada, though there have been tragedies and wars, the country is so big and fresh and full of promise."

"It is not very polite of you to talk thus," Anne chided smilingly. "Visitors are surely expected to go into raptures and declare they have nothing in the least degree resembling it at home."

"That is certainly true." He was smiling at her. "In Europe, I have found something I did not have at home, and I cannot imagine how I contrived to live without it until now."

"Doctor—"

"I wish you would call me Edouard," he interrupted.

"I couldn't possibly! We scarcely know each other," she exclaimed.

"I will admit our meeting was unconventional," he agreed, "but on board ship friendships often spring up."

"We are not on board ship now."

"But we are still friends, I hope? I would be pleased to have you call me by my given name."

Probably she was making too much of the matter, far more than a real sewing maid would make. "Edouard, then, and my name is Anna—though I prefer to shorten it to Anne."

"I am happy to make your acquaintance, Anne." He shook hands with her solemnly, his blue eyes twinkling. "What were we talking about?"

"I'm sure it wasn't important. What other places have we time to see?"

"The Louvre. We cannot possibly see all of it, but, if you like paintings, there are some fine ones there."

"You will be bored, having to go round with me if you have already seen everything," she protested.

"On the contrary," he demurred, "it will give me even greater pleasure to show them to you and discover if your tastes match with my own."

She was both pleased and regretful to find that they did, both of them disliking the sentimental Watteaus and admiring the work of David. It was agreeable to be with someone with whom she could so quickly forge bands of friendship but it was necessary to remind herself that soon he would be leaving France altogether. It was not wise to allow their mutual liking to drift into anything deeper.

"It is late!" She spotted a clock on a tower as they came out into the open again. "I think I should start back to the chateau. I am allowed so much the disposal of my own time that I don't like to take unfair advantage."

"Notre Dame and the Luxembourg Palace will have to wait for another time then. There will be another time, I hope?" He was looking at her in a manner she could only describe to herself as tenderly hopeful, and his hand clasped her own.

"Naturally, if my duties permit, I shall be very glad to accept your escort," she said primly.

"I'll get the trap."

"You cannot mean to drive me all the way to the chateau and then make the return journey?" she said. "It is much too fatiguing!"

"Certainly, you do not believe I would leave you to walk the entire way back by yourself! It's less than an hour's drive, and I don't want to lose one moment of your company," he declared.

There was something irresistibly frank and disarming about his open admiration. As they walked back to the stables, she found herself regretting more and more keenly that their friendship must be of such short duration. When she returned to England and confessed her adventure to her uncle, she doubted if any of the young men he produced as possible suitors would match this charming young physician.

"I quite forgot to tell you." They were trotting out of the city as she turned to him. "Berthe told me something about the lady who owns the park we were in. According to Berthe, who may be exaggerating or have gained the wrong impression, for she had the tale from one of the gardeners, a Countess du Bois who is disordered in her wits owns the entire property."

"You are not seeking another patient for me, are you?" he enquired.

"Of course not! But Berthe told me the poor lady dresses as if Marie-Antoinette still lived, and she never leaves the chateau. The park where the children can play was made in memory of her daughter, who was guillotined during the Terror."

"The inscription we saw on the fountain?" he remembered. "It sounds as if the story might be true. Do you want to drive into the park on our way? We pass by it."

"I know. I noticed this morning and meant to mention the tale then, but I was so excited about going to Paris with you that it went out of my head," she confessed.

To her surprise, he put back his head and laughed, exclaiming, "I am so glad you are not a rich, fashionable young lady who would die before she admitted that she was actually looking forward to anything!"

"You don't approve of rich, fashionable young ladies?"

"Not much." His expression was wry. "Oh, we have them in Québec, languid, high-nosed beauties who simper behind their fans and find life too utterly exhausting for words! For myself I have no patience with pretence or affectation. The quality I admire most in a woman is honesty."

"Oh," said Anne in a small voice.

"It will not delay you for long if you wish to see the park again," he said persuasively.

"Could we drive round a little distance? It would be interesting to see the chateau—if it can be seen from the road?"

"This lane might bring us to the private grounds." He turned the pony's head into the leafy alley, guiding it skillfully over the ruts. At each side, high walls hid the views around, and, behind the walls, trees bowed sideways to the breeze.

"There's a bridge ahead," Anne pointed out.

There the walls dipped down sufficiently for them to be able to see over their tops. To their right were the roundabout and swings, where a few children were still swinging while their nurses gossiped on the benches. On the left, beyond the trees and bushes, the pointed roofs of a large building could be glimpsed.

"That must be the Château du Bois, where the countess lives," Anne said.

"The *mad* countess," Edouard said.

"It does sound rather far-fetched, doesn't it?" she agreed. "But it would be interesting to go there."

"With a view to spring cleaning the entire house?" His eyes were teasing. "I suspect that you are somewhat of a managing woman, Miss Anne!"

"I am beginning to suspect that I must be," she said ruefully. "It is a most unattractive trait, I fear."

"I have not yet found an unattractive trait in you," he said. "Forgive me if that sounds a little—well, presumptuous. It is not intended so."

"I do not take it so," she said and felt a slow blush rising in her cheeks.

"There is a gate beyond the bridge. This lane probably divides the property and skirts the outer walls to bring us onto the highway again," he said, tactfully changing the subject and urging the pony onward.

The bridge was prettily rustic, with ivy trailing over the curved parapet. The sun, sinking lower in a rose tinted sky, cast radiance over the waters of a narrow stream that ran beneath. From the other side of the wall could be heard the squeals of the children as they bounced and swung.

"That must be the chateau." Anne turned her head to look through the bars of a padlocked gate up a curving avenue of chestnut trees beyond which could be seen the façade of a turreted stone building.

"Everything looks well kept." Edouard nodded towards the neatly trimmed grass between the trees, the raked gravel of the long avenue.

"Someone is coming down the steps." Anne had glimpsed a dark figure walking slowly. It was not near enough for any features to be discerned, but it was possible to see the wide spreading, black skirt and what appeared to be black plumes on the lady's head.

"I suspect this is your countess," Edouard said.

The figure, having reached the bottom of the steps, continued to walk slowly towards them. A tall, slim woman with white hair piled high, her movements stately under the panniered dress. There was, even at a distance, an air of great dignity about her. Her face was still a blur when she paused, raising her head like a deer scenting trouble on the wind, and then turning, went swiftly back the way she had come.

"She must have seen us," Anne said, disappointed.

"And did not care for what she saw," Edouard said ruefully.

"She was not near enough to see anything. I suppose she simply avoids everybody."

"Which may be proof of discrimination rather than madness." He clicked his tongue at the pony, and it began to walk on again.

"She was certainly wearing an old-fashioned dress," Anne said.

"Those huge skirts must be monstrously hot in summer," he remarked.

"But very splendid. This land does wind back to the highway, as you thought."

"I have a reasonably good sense of direction." He slanted a glance towards her. "At this moment, I wish it were not so, that I might, with honesty, claim to be lost and so enjoy your company for longer."

"Now you are flattering me," she began, but he shook his head.

"I am a busy man with neither the time nor the inclination to flatter the ladies. Between us there is perfect honesty. I feel it instinctively."

His instinct was at fault then, Anne thought, and began to feel downcast again. It was not really in her nature to deceive, and what had begun as an impulsive bid for independence on her part, was now threatening to involve her in endless complications.

"Will you come to Paris again next week?" he asked as they drove towards the Château Lanuit. "I have yet to show you Notre Dame."

"I doubt if I am entitled to take time off again so soon," she said doubtfully. "In four weeks, perhaps."

"Four weeks from today—if you wish to come. But that is a long time."

She wished very much to come. Too much, she reflected, for if she allowed herself to become too fond of Edouard, it would hurt the more when he had to return. And if it became necessary to confess her deception, then it would be even more painful.

"Four weeks from today," she said meekly.

By then, she would have been here for almost two months and would have controlled the queer, excited feelings that rose up on her when she thought of Edouard.

The gates stood open and they bowled up the drive, to be greeted by the two children who came rushing along the terrace and down the steps in what was clearly a state of high excitement.

"Papa has returned!" Justine was jumping up and down, her cheeks scarlet. "He has brought many rolls of silk and velvet and he wishes us to have new clothes! You will have to make them."

"Say 'good afternoon' to Monsieur le docteur," Anne chided, alighting from the trap.

"You are a real doctor?" Gaston looked suspicious.

"A very real one," Edouard informed him.

"Perhaps he has come to see maman." Justine put her thumb in her mouth and stared at him. "Have you come to see maman?"

"Not unless your maman has sent for me." Edouard turned to clasp Anne's hand and mount to the driving seat again.

"Mademoiselle Sayle!" The baron's voice checked them as he strode through the main door and came down the steps. He was still clad in boots and travelling cloak, the deepset eyes in the heavy, handsome face ringed with the effects of either fatigue or dissipation.

"Make the physician visit maman," Justine said shrilly.

"You are Doctor—?"

"De Reynard, sir." Edouard bowed slightly in answer to the question. "I am a visitor to France and have not yet hung out my shingle."

"But you are fully qualified?"

"Yes. I gained my medical degree in Québec."

"Your parents were emigrés?"

"From Paris." There was a faint coolness in Edouard's tone. He clearly did not relish being questioned as if he were a tradesman.

The baron seemed to sense it, for his next remark

was uttered rather less abruptly. "It is not my intention to intrude upon your leisure time, Doctor de Reynard, but my wife, having heard your name, has it firmly fixed in her head that she wishes to consult you. As her condition is a chronic one, I doubt very much if your remedies are any more efficacious than those recommended by her own physicians, but naturally, she would be pleased to see a new face and obtain a new opinion."

"If the baroness wishes to consult me—" Edouard hesitated and then nodded. "I would be willing to talk to her."

"Would it be convenient for you to do so now or does pressing business hasten you back to Paris?" the baron asked.

"Now would be convenient," Edouard said.

"Then I will conduct you to the baroness." He gave Anne a nod in which she discerned a hint of disapproval, though she could not ascertain its cause, and the two men went up the steps together.

"Perhaps maman will not die," Justine said, gazing after them.

"Of course she will not!" Anne scolded. "The physician from Québec will probably think up some treatment that will make her perfectly well again."

"Are you going to marry him?" Justine enquired as Anne mounted the steps.

Anne, feeling the threat of a blush, opened her mouth, but Gaston spoke first.

"Of course she is not!" he said scornfully. "She is here to work for us."

"Which I will spend most of the days doing if you are all to have new garments," Anne said briskly. "Where did your papa put the material he brought?"

"Berthe took it up to your room," Gaston told her.

"Then we will go and see what is there." Anne climbed the stairs, wrenching her mind away from all thoughts of Edouard's agreeable company.

There was a great deal there. It looked as if the baron had ransacked every shop in Paris, Anne thought, as she beheld the rolls of silk, satin, brocade, and velvet. There was sufficient work for half a dozen seamstresses. Silently she blessed the fact that styles were so simple, else she would have been forced to admit that she was not a skilled dressmaker at all. Had panniers still been in fashion, she would have been unable to do the necessary cutting, swathing, and pleating.

"You are to make a gown for maman," Gaston said. "Papa has determined to hold a ball. There has not been a ball here since my sister was born."

"A ball?" Anne, her fingers busily unwinding a roll of silvery muslin, looked up with interest.

"In one month's time," Justine chimed in. "We are to be allowed to go."

"Sweetheart, you are too young to go to balls!" Anne said.

"I am not too young to go if papa says, and papa did say!" Justine said stubbornly. "Maman is going too. I heard papa say, 'Sophie if you don't wish me to bring another governess into this household you had better find some cure for your ailments. Sick or no, you will attend the ball and play your rightful part as hostess!' "

Which explained why Edouard had been summoned to attend the baroness, Anne thought, fingering a length of lavendar silk patterned with tiny stars. The delicate colour would provide a foil for the baroness's chestnut hair—if she actually attended this ball. It would be an ordeal for someone who had been confined to her chambers for six years.

"What dress will you make for me?" Justine was demanding.

"This one." Anne chose a length of spotted white muslin. "And I shall make a long sash of cherry velvet ribbon. It will look beautiful—provided you wash your face and comb your hair."

"I shall wash myself all over," the little girl announced with dignity.

"A splendid idea!" The baron's voice sounded from the door. "Your supper is ready, so you had better run along."

There was a moment's hesitation as the boy's eyes, too shrewd and aware for a child of nine, darted between his father and Anne.

Quickly she said, "Has my friend, Doctor de Reynard, left?"

"A few moments since. You wished to speak with him?"

"He invited me to visit Paris with him in four weeks time, and I hoped to confirm that I could go."

"It is already confirmed," the baron said.

Out of the corner of her eye Anne saw that Gaston and Justine were leaving the room. Apparently a sewing maid who had an admirer was unlikely to turn into a dreaded governess.

"I hope the consultation was of some value," she said primly.

"It may have been." The baron sounded moody. "I will regard it as a medical miracle if so, for Sophie must have consulted a dozen physicians during these past years."

"The children tell me there is to be a ball."

"It is high time that we began to entertain again according to our station," he said impatiently. "Sophie has neglected her duties for too long."

"Sir, it is really not fitting for you to speak to me about your wife or for me to listen," Anne said uncomfortably. "If you will excuse me—"

"You think me a bad husband?" He raised his dark brows and looked sourly amused. "Is it not the wife who makes the husband what he is?"

"I am not married, sir, and cannot give an opinion."

"Oh, you will be married soon enough, I daresay," he said. "You came here and turned my household inside out, shaking us up like feathers in a pillow case, and you will not be content until you are shaking up your own household! If that young physician has any senses, he will take to his heels and run as fast as he can, but, of course, he has no sense! You will, of course, attend the ball."

"Of course I will not attend the ball!" she retorted, too startled to be polite. "What would your neighbours think to see your sewing maid among the guests?"

"You are promoted to housekeeper. Make yourself a gown out of this." He turned and pulled a roll of pale emerald silk from the other rolls.

"Sir, when housekeepers attend balls they wear black and sit in the corner—which is what I would do anyway since I am not fond of dancing. It is quite out of the question!"

"The baroness wishes it. You may invite your physician friend also. You must remember, Mademoiselle Sayle, that you are now in the land of liberty, equality, and fraternity!"

"I doubt if that applies to sewing maids," Anne said wryly.

"But you, my dear Mademoiselle, are no mere

sewing maid. There is about you a natural hauteur, an air of authority—"

"I have had the benefit of a little education, and a natural talent for aping my betters!"

"Wear the green!" He thrust the emerald silk towards her and strode out, leaving her staring after him.

= 5 =

"BUT OF COURSE you must attend the ball, Mademoiselle!"

The Baroness Sophie spoke with unusual decision, her eyes less heavily shadowed than usual. "I insist upon your being there and bringing Doctor de Reynard."

"His treatment appears to be doing some good, Madame?" Anne ventured.

Edouard had visited the chateau, but Anne had missed him, having walked into the village to buy some silk thread. In the shop, the woman who served her had been voluble on the subject of the forthcoming ball.

"*Tiens!* but I cannot even remember when the poor baroness was well enough to entertain! The baron seeks his pleasures in Paris now, they tell me! What it is to have money! But now the chateau has been cleaned and refurbished, and they say the baroness will attend the ball."

"Certainly she will, for she is the hostess," Anne had said crisply as she took her leave.

Now, looking at the baroness, she was aware of a decided improvement, not only in the lady herself but in her surroundings. The shutters were partly open, the chamber had been dusted and tidied, and the baroness had exchanged her couch for a high-backed armchair.

"Your friend's treatment consists of no treatment at all," the other said. "He informs me that I do not require physic but that my diet is deficient in iron, so I must partake of vegetables and fruit, coarse bread, and lightly chopped liver. I must drink red wine with honey in it, open my window when the sun is shining, and walk a little farther each day."

"It must be efficacious," Anne said, and broke off as she saw the other's expression.

"You insist you are not a governess, and yet you use such words as that," the baroness said suspiciously.

"I believe I already told you that I have received some education from Miss Turnbull, but certainly not sufficient to warrant my teaching anybody anything," Anne said. "But, if you will forgive me for saying so, the children do need the service of a governess."

"So that my husband can humiliate me by seducing her? You look shocked, Mademoiselle, but that is the truth. The other servants know it—even the children are aware of it! I have made it clear that on the day another governess is brought into this house I will leave it, even if I have be be carried out! All men are brutes, interested in one thing alone, and I will not run the risk of bearing another child!" Scarlet dyed her cheeks, and her voice was shrill.

Anne, crimson herself at the frankness of the other's revelation, said, "Madame, I do beg you to talk to Doctor de Reynard about this. He may be able to suggest—there may be some remedy."

"Perhaps." The baroness looked doubtful and then unexpectedly smiled. "I wonder what it is about you, Mademoiselle, that leads one to confide in you? I never spoke so intimately with a servant before. I never spoke to intimately with anyone!"

Later, she would probably regret it, Anne thought, as she curtsied and withdrew. The baroness was a woman swayed by the impulse of the moment. By the time the ball was held, she would wonder what had led her into including a sewing maid among her guests.

Meanwhile there was no denying that the entire chateau seemed to have sprung to life. Everywhere one turned gleaming floors and windows, sparkling crystal and polished wood met the eye. The servants seemed to move briskly about their tasks, and, from the terrace, clipped lawns and weeded flower beds stretched to the drive.

Anne herself had worked harder than she had ever worked in her life. The days had been filled with cutting and sewing until she thought privately that she would scream if she saw one more seam to be basted or length of lace to be gathered into a frill. In the evenings, she had forced herself to ignore aching back and fingers and work on the novel. It would be only a slender volume, but the writing of it was giving her a great deal of trouble, for the beautifully rounded sentences that formed in her mind limped onto the paper, and the heroine, whom she had envisaged as the model of an independent, energetic female, seemed quite determined to waste a lot of sentimental emotion on a physician who had crept into the tale from somewhere.

On the following day, she was to meet Edouard and spend a few hours with him in the capital. It would make a pleasant diversion, she considered, and told herself firmly it was no more than that. When he returned to Québec, their acquaintanceship must cease, since she would be resuming her real life. And the prospect of that depressed her so much that she put down the sleeve she was hemming and reached for her cloak. A walk would raise her spirits and make her more cheerful. One of the great advantages of being a servant was that one could dispense with chaperones.

She made her way down the drive, passed through the gate, and turned in the direction of the park. The highway was quiet, there being few travellers so soon after the midday meal, and she walked briskly, enjoying the breeze on her face and the sounds of birdsong in the trees at each side of the road.

When the roundabout and swings came into view, she turned into the lane where she and Edouard had driven and, impelled by some instinct stronger than curiosity, followed its windings to the bridge and the locked gate beyond. If the Countess du Bois chose to retreat from reality into a past where her daughter had still been alive, then it was none of her business, Anne reasoned sensibly, but the gates beyond which the chateau lay drew her like a magnet.

What she did not expect, as she approached them, was the liveried figure, complete with knee breeches and powdered wig, who emerged and informed her, "You are to go up to the chateau. Madame will see you."

"I beg your pardon?" Anne stared at the man.

"The countess will receive you," he repeated impatiently. "You were seen approaching, and I was sent to open the gate."

Anne, bewildered, stepped through, feeling as if she were stepping into a dream. The possibility that it might turn out to be a nightmare if the countess was truly insane crossed her mind, but she dismissed it impatiently. She had never been one to shrink from an unexpected adventure, and she had no intention of beginning now.

"I'm to wait," the footman said. "Go on up to the chateau."

Presumably she was to be let out again. She nodded smilingly and, with more show of confidence than she was actually feeling, walked up the drive between the towering oaks. The carved grey stone of the turreted building, with its curving flights of steps running to a central balcony off which a deeply recessed main door opened, had about it the grandeur of a bygone age. Mounting the steps, she would not have been surprised to look up and behold a knight in armour silhouetted in one of the long windows flanking the entrance. The door, however, was opened by another liveried footman, who silently indicated an antechamber at the other side of a hall lit by sunlight, which pierced the windows and created lozenges of gold on the stone floor.

The anteroom was similarly austere, the stone unrelieved by any hangings or pictures. The two chairs and table were of dark wood. Anne stood, her eyes moving round the chamber, her heart beating uncomfortably fast. There was the tapping of heels across the hall, and the stately figure she had previously glimpsed at a distance hove into view, pausing for an instant to stare at her through the open door, then entering as Anne dropped a curtsey.

Close to, the countess was equally as impressive as she had been from afar; her tall figure exaggerated by high heeled shoes, the wide panniers of her black dress, the white hair—not all of it could be her own!—stretched over a towering concoction of black velvet from which a long veil hung to the hem of her skirt. She was clearly old, though she held herself erect, and the lines on her face were camouflaged with a thick layer of paint.

"I saw you before, outside the gates," she began without greeting. "I assume you have been instructed to deliver the invitation."

"Invitation, Madame?" Anne said blankly.

"To the Lanuit ball. There is to be a ball, is there

not? Or has the gossip in the neighbourhood been inaccurate?"

"There is to be a ball in two weeks' time, Madame."

"And you are not here with an invitation for me? The Lanuits are not troubling to invite one of their most distinguished neighbours?"

"I understand," Anne said carefully, "that the baron and baroness are under the impression that you do not go out into society."

"In that they are correct, since there is no social life worth the effort of attending," the countess said dryly. "The excuse you offer is a tactful one. I suspect they are chary of inviting one who is disordered in her wits."

"Madame—" Anne broke off, embarrassed by the shrewdness in the other's handsome, painted face.

"You are Mademoiselle Anna Sayle? My servants keep me informed of the gossip in the district. What they have been unable to determine is whether or not you are Jean Lanuit's mistress yet."

"Indeed I am not, Madame, nor ever likely to be," Anne said coldly.

"If that is true then you have considerable strength of character, though one must admit you do not possess the porcelain prettiness that usually attracts gentlemen. Well, when you return to the Chateau Lanuit you may inform your employers that, since they have decided to begin entertaining again, I intend to grace the occasion with my presence, and I shall expect a formal invitation."

"Yes, Madame." Anne essayed another curtsey.

"I have not yet given you leave to depart," the countess said. "Since it appears you are not here to deliver an invitation, why are you here at all?"

"I was taking a walk."

"In the middle of the day? Small wonder society is in such a state when maidservants wander at their leisure. However, I am informed that you are not in the usual mould of servant girls."

"And you, Madame," Anne heard herself retorting, "are not in the usual mould of countesses!"

To her astonishment and relief the old lady laughed, creakingly, as if she were out of the habit. "And you have spirit and the typical English determination not to be bullied."

"It accounts for our vanquishing Napoleon."

"It accounts for nothing of the sort!" the countess declared. "That Corsican and his two silly wives were all upstarts in my opinion! True nobility cannot be learned or wrested from other hands. His Majesty King Louis was a shambling creature, more interested in mending clocks than in reforming his government, but he had more true dignity in his little finger than Bonaparte had in his whole body."

"They must have been wonderful times!" Anne could not help exclaiming.

"Settled times, before all this nonsense of equality," the countess said. "People knew their place. Oh, there were injustices, but the malcontents replaced them with worse injustices of their own. Is it to be wondered at that I have stopped the clock in this household at a time when I was most happy?"

"Yet you opened the park, Madame," Anne said.

"I am—fond of children." A fleeting shadow sped across the heavily painted face. "I—had a daughter once. Perhaps you have seen the fountain with her name inscribed upon it?"

"Yes, Madame. I was—curious."

" 'Toinette was my only child, named for the queen. I was widowed when she was only twelve, and, from then on, I devoted my life to her. She was very lovely, and her dowry was considerable. I had hopes of matching her with the highest, but I was in no hurry to see her wed. Her companionship was very sweet."

Her voice trailed away. It was plain that she had forgotten she was talking to a servant, but was back in the days when the monarchy had ruled and there had been apparent stability, all swept away by the Revolution. Then, as if she had been recalled to the present abruptly, she gave a little shake of her head, and resumed in a hard, dry tone from which all emotion had been squeezed.

"When the Revolution began, my daughter, like many young, idealistic people, regarded it as something to be desired, a way of ridding France of old corruptions! We—quarrelled about that as we had sometimes quarrelled about other things. 'Toinette was headstrong, intolerant of what she regarded as outworn tradition. I myself was arrested in the summer of seventeen ninety-three. I was held in the Luxembourg Prison for more than a year. I heard that my daughter had also been arrested. Her support for the Jacobins availed her nothing, since she was an aristocrat. When I was released, I made enquiry and learned she had been guillotined in the spring of seventeen ninety-four. She was not quite twenty-five years old. I returned here. The chateau had been looted but not destroyed, and I still had an adequate income. I have lived here ever since. The amusement park is 'Toinette's memorial. For the rest—the clocks are stopped and I refuse to become a part of the shoddy vulgarity of this so-called new era."

"I am very sorry, Madame," Anne said.

"Why should you be?" the old lady asked tartly. "You never knew 'Toinette nor experienced the horrors of a world ripped apart by violence and greed. In England your monarch may be mad, but your government seems stable enough! Do you have a family there?"

"I'm an orphan, Madame."

"But you clearly received some education. You do not speak or comport yourself in the general manner of a servant."

"I was at a school—an academy for young ladies. I attended classes there."

"Your French is excellent—a little deficient in pronunciation, but one seldom gets that from a foreigner. You may go now. I shall expect my official invitation within a few days."

Anne curtsied and went out into the hall. The countess was not mad, she reflected as she descended the steps. She was only sour and grieving for a child and a time that would never come again. Yet she was not immune to ordinary human curiosity. She was determined to attend the ball at the Chateau Lanuit in order to find out for herself if the rumours concerning the health of the baroness and the behaviour of the baron were true.

Anne was let out through the gate by the footman. The countess must pay high wages in order to persuade her domestics into wearing out-of-date clothes, she thought, as she recrossed the bridge and hurried up the lane.

When she reached the Chateau Lanuit she saw, with some surprise, the baroness seated in a wicker chair on the terrace, a large sunbonnet on her head, and a shawl about her shoulders.

"It is such a warm afternoon," she greeted Anne, "that I have risked taking the air. You have been for a walk?"

"To the park, Madame, where I was bidden into the Château du Bois," Anne told her.

"You went to see the mad countess!" Gaston, who was spinning a top on the paving stones near his mother, looked up excitedly.

"She is not mad," Anne said, "only sad and rather lonely. It seems that she has tired of her long isolation, Madame, and expects an invitation to the ball."

"The countess coming here? Oh, but how is she to be received?" The baroness began to look very agitated.

"I am sure she will be an added attraction to the proceedings," the baron observed, coming round the corner in time to hear his wife's words. "You actually spoke to her, Mademoiselle?"

"I was invited to the chateau," Anne said. "She appeared under the impression that I was on my way there with an invitation."

"Why, we never even considered it," the baroness said, fluttering. "We have never actually met her. Very few people have, as far as I know."

"Her servants keep her informed about events in the district," Anne said. "She was interested to hear about the ball."

"And naturally expects to attend. Well, it is more than six years since we last entertained on any scale, so one trusts she will not be disappointed in the quality of the entertainment," the baron said. "You had better write out an invitation at once, Sophie, and I'll have one of the grooms take it round."

"But how can one be expected to converse with her?" the baroness complained. "What is one going to say?"

"The usual social pleasantries, I imagine. I am sure you will cope magnificently, my dear." He sounded slightly impatient.

"It is so long since we had company. I cannot imagine what put the idea of a ball into our heads," she returned fretfully.

"I fancy that we must blame the bustling English mademoiselle for that," the baron answered. "She has taken us all by the heels and shaken us up! Do try not to get into a panic! All you have to do is look charming and make the appropriate noises."

"But there will be dancing too."

"It would be a somewhat peculiar ball if there were no dancing," he said dryly.

"I don't believe I am strong enough to dance," she said plaintively.

"You will certainly be strong enough to open the ball by partnering me." There was more command than reassurance in his voice. "When that duty is performed, you may sit down in comfort for the rest of the evening. Mademoiselle Sayle, be so good as to take the children elsewhere. It must be some time since they enjoyed the benefit of some English conversation!"

He sounded thoroughly disgruntled, and with some excuse. A sewing maid, Anne thought as she hastily beckoned the children, had no business to stand listening to a private altercation between her employers. Yet she was sorry for the baron, who was clearly worried lest his wife would not be able to fulfil her social duties adequately.

"Why is papa so cross?" Justine demanded plaintively as soon as they were out of earshot.

"He is not cross, sweetheart," Anne soothed. "He is anxious about your maman."

"Perhaps maman will not die so soon," the little girl said, "since she now begins to come out of her room."

"Your maman is in no danger of dying," Anne said firmly. "Her health is improving."

"And perhaps the Countess du Bois is not really mad?" Gaston said.

"She is possibly a little eccentric—you know the word?"

"You are not supposed to be teaching us words!" The suspicious frown was back in his eyes.

"We do not only learn from governesses," Anne said mildly. "Your maman learned from the physician how to improve her health."

"Are you going to be married to him?" Justine enquired.

"He is a friend," Anne said, but she was blushing.

"If you do marry him," Gaston said, with an air of making amends for his former sulkiness, "we shall be very glad for you and very sorry for us."

"I am not expecting to marry anybody for a very long time, if ever," Anne said. "Now, shall we go to the kitchen and find out if Monsieur Louis has any of those little iced cakes to spare?"

The children nodded and ran ahead of her. They still had moments of suspicion, but they had largely accepted her, she reflected. They even made considerable efforts to appear clean and tidy. But they needed a firmer hand than her own and a better education than the irregular instruction given by the village priest. It was selfish of their parents to be so wrapped up in their own problems that they had no time to spare for their children.

"Mademoiselle!" The baron's voice halted her.

"Sir?" She turned, seeing him hurrying down the corridor towards her. For some reason his bulky frame, dark against the sunlight slanting through the open door, made her nervous. It was as if someone had flicked open a shutter in some dark recess of her mind, then slammed it down before she could see what lay beyond.

"I have the invitation for the countess." He held it out. "I would like you to take it round to the chateau now."

"You want *me* to take it?" Anne looked at him in some surprise.

"Since you appear to have met and talked with her, I would prefer you to deliver it rather than one of the other servants."

"Yes, of course."

"I was—somewhat sharp with you just now." He cleared his throat, frowning. "My wife is apt to fuss unnecessarily, and I am consequently inclined to be impatient with her. It irritates me that the children should witness any conflict between us."

"Children are usually aware of a very great deal," Anne said.

"Doubtless you are right. You have not forgotten that I wish you to attend this ball? In that, at least, Sophie and I are in accord."

"The baroness very kindly gave me leave to invite Doctor de Reynard to partner me."

"Ah! the worthy young physician!" The baron's lips curled slightly. "Do you bring him as companion or protector?"

"I do not anticipate requiring protection while I am beneath your roof," she said quellingly.

"A young woman of decided mettle!" He stood looking down at her, blocking her retreat.

"A sewing maid with a smattering of education. No more than that, sir."

"Mademoiselle! Don't you want cake?" Justine had come running up from the kitchen. Seeing her father, she hesitated.

"I have an errand to perform," Anne said, "but your papa would greatly relish a slice of Monsieur Louis's cake, I believe." Taking the invitation from his hand, she bobbed a curtsey and went out through the farther door.

The baron, she thought, had not given up hope of seducing her, not because she attracted him, but because he was the kind of man whose pride could not endure that any female should remain indifferent to him. Her own feelings puzzled her. She felt not the slightest inclination to yield to his blandishments, but, in his presence, she was aware of an emotion within herself that was part fear and part excitement. It was as if his existence stirred some long buried memory.

She shook off the feeling and walked more briskly to the gate and along the highway. She was quite sure that someone at the Château du Bois would have remarked her arrival and, as she crossed the bridge, she saw that the gate stood ajar and the powdered and bewigged footman was waiting.

"Madame wishes you to go up," he said. Not by the flicker of a muscle did he betray any surprise at his mistress admitting someone from the outside world twice in one day.

Climbing the steps for the second time, Anne thought ruefully that it was as well she was fond of exercise, since it now looked as if running errands was yet another of her duties.

The countess was seated in one of the high-backed chairs in the antechamber. Though she was old, her hands, on which several rings glinted, were still beautiful. She launched into speech as she had done before, without greeting. "I will write my acceptance while you wait."

"You knew I would return this afternoon?" Anne said.

"I thought it more than likely that the baron, who

clearly wishes to reinstate himself in the good graces of the neighbourhood, would not wish to offend me," the countess said. "Also I am quite certain that he and his wife are anxious to meet me. It is nearly a quarter of a century since I left my estate. Are you truly a mere sewing maid?"

"I am employed as such, but my duties do seem to be somewhat wider in scope."

"But you are not one of that sorry procession of so-called governesses?"

"No, Madame."

"One cannot blame him, I suppose." The countess had risen and crossed to a small escritoire, where she began to write. "His wife, from all accounts, objected to the realities of the marriage bed and took refuge in invalidism. A man must satisfy his appetites, but he should not do so on his own doorstep. That displays bad breeding."

She was talking with the same freedom that had startled Anne before. She thought now that she understood it better. Great ladies chatted freely before servants because to them servants' opinions and reactions were entirely unimportant.

"When I saw you first," the countess said, blotting what she had written and reaching for the sealing wax, "you were being driven by a young man."

"By Doctor de Reynard, Madame."

"The physician who has been called in to treat the baroness? Yes, my servants informed me of that also. What were you doing riding around with him?"

"Begging your pardon," Anne said, "but I believe my friendships are my own affair."

"You are remarkably insolent." The countess straightened up and stared at her.

"Insolence is not always confined to the lower classes."

"Meaning that I am a meddling old woman!" The countess uttered a bark of laughter. "I have little else to do save observe the goings-on of those who have not left the world behind. I am not, however, ill-disposed towards people. It merely occurred to me that an intelligent girl like yourself might count it as a feather in her cap to capture the affections of a rising young physician. Or were you merely discussing the treatment he has recommended for the baroness?"

Despite her indignation, Anne found herself smiling. The countess shamelessly used her age and her rank as an excuse for what was actually impertinence, but she was clearly not malicious.

"I met Edo—the physician on the Channel crossing," she explained. "He lives in Canada and will be returning there in a few weeks. We struck up a friendship, that's all."

"And you expect the friendship to terminate when he sets sail again? You have not thought of bettering yourself by marriage to him?"

"I have—he has not precisely asked me yet," Anne stammered.

"Oh, I have small doubt that he will." The countess handed her the sealed parchment and returned to her chair. "I am informed that in the New World everything moves twice as fast as it does here. And you are precisely the kind of energetic young woman who ought to be married to an ambitious man on the verge of a professional career. As he has the 'de' in his name, I assume he has a title?"

"He does not care to use it."

"Remarkably foolish of him! The 'de' would have entitled him to the use of a footstool in the presence of the monarchy! However, the young must move with the times, I suppose. If he proposes, I would advise you to accept. You are not likely to receive a better offer, and such a marriage might prove beneficial to both of you."

"It is very kind of you to take an interest," Anne began.

"It is not in the least kind," the countess interrupted. "It is merely that I have seen too often the misfortunes that arise when the wrong people marry each other! However, you are not bound to take my advice. Young girls always imagine they are wiser than their elders and go their own way, indifferent to the pain they may cause!"

Her eyes and voice were suddenly bleak and remote. Then she shook her white head and said curtly, "You may return with my answer, Mademoiselle. It will give me pleasure to attend the Lanuit ball."

"Madame."

Anne curtsied again and withdrew, crossing the austere, stone-flagged hall to the door. There was, she sensed, more than grief in this house. There was a loneliness of spirit that had its roots in the past, in some event of which she was ignorant. She walked slowly down the steps and between the sheltering oaks to the gate where the footman waited.

The sound of children's voices came from the park. Crossing the bridge, Anne paused to look over the wall at the brightly painted roundabout and the swings. She could see the fountain over which the mermaid presided, frozen in green stone, never growing older. Like 'Tointette du Bois, who had not been twenty-five years of age when she had kept her appointment with Madame Guillotine. Edouard was right. There were still too many sad and violent echoes from the past here in France. To begin life in a new and vibrant society would be an exciting challenge. It was a challenge she would have welcomed, had the circumstances been different, but they were against her. She was not Anna Sayle who could better herself by marrying an ambitious physician. She was Anne Sinclair, heiress to a fortune and the daughter of a lord. The Honourable Anne Sinclair to be exact. And her behaviour had been anything but honourable.

She had, on a whim, delayed her entry into polite society and deceived everybody for what she now feared had been a selfish bid to clutch at a few weeks' independence. If Edouard ever found out what she had done, he would be grievously disappointed, for he had made it clear that he considered honesty the highest virtue in a woman.

As she walked soberly back to the highway, her conscience smote her with a fresh pang. Since coming to France, she had not paused to consider how Anna was faring in the invidious position she had been placed.

II
Anna

= 1 =

Sinclair House,
Yorkshire.
Tuesday.

MY DEAR ANNE,

This is the first letter I have ever penned to you, so I hope we may dispense with formality and use Christian names? I have decided to write to you once a week. I will not post them immediately but wait until I have four or five, then send a bundle all together. On the other hand, I may not send them at all. What I am trying to do is make sense of my own thoughts and feelings, which, at the best of times, are apt to be woefully muddled and chaotic. At least I always obtained high marks in the English composition class, so I need not fear your criticism on that score—though you have never been in the least censorious!

I do not know if you can begin to imagine my feelings when I boarded the stage, wearing your dress and with your luggage. Oh, I am sure you, too, were struggling with excitement and anxiety, but you, having been the instigator of our plan, had the comfort of knowing yourself to be more mistress of the occasion. I have never had your energy or courage and, as I sat in the couch, I found myself half-wishing that Miss Turnbull had accompanied us to Plymouth, thus making our change of identities impossible.

The journey seemed very long, though I was naturally interested in the changing views as we travelled eastward towards London. I thought how dreadful it would be—but also how exciting! if we were attacked by footpads. However no footpads came within screaming distance, and, by early evening, having made good time, we bowled into the capital. Everything was noise and bustle, torches flaring, relatives greeting relatives and boys grabbing at the horses' reins and demanding twopence for carrying one's luggage. I had no fear of looking bewildered because most people were looking bewildered!

A respectable looking woman with grey hair and a comfortably round figure stepped forward as we passengers alighted, scanning each face. I took a chance and said to her, "Dorcas? Mistress Dorcas Grant?"

"Why, Miss Anne, fancy your remembering me!" she exclaimed. "I declare that I'd have passed by and not known you. You've grown that pretty! I've a boy to see to the baggage, and we've a chamber reserved at the inn."

Her words put me into a sad fluster, for though you had told me that a Dorcas Grant would be meeting me, you never said she'd known you before. Perhaps you didn't remember.

"It's been a long time," I said lamely.

"Eight years," she replied at once. "That was a sad time, Miss Anne, and it near broke my heart to leave the West Country, but I'd not have been contented to work for the new tenants. And Lord Sinclair was good enough to offer me employment up north, so I took it, but I've never stopped thinking about you and hoping we'd meet again."

She was urging me across the yard towards the entrance of the inn where a sign hung.

"You ought to have written to me," I began and realised immediately that I had said the wrong thing, for she turned her head and gave me a very puzzled look.

"Surely you haven't forgotten that I never learned reading or writing?" she said.

"To tell you the truth I've forgotten nearly everything," I said.

"Put it out of your mind more like and small blame to you," she said. I wondered what she meant by that, but we had entered the inn, and the maidservant was showing us into a very clean and decent bedchamber with two beds in it.

"I've ordered a supper, Miss Anne, to be served in a little private parlour downstairs," Dorcas told me. "There's hot water for you to sponge your face and hands."

She was fussing round me like a mother hen with one chick, but she was still puzzled. I could tell by the quick glances that she kept shooting at me. Finally she said, "I still cannot get over how prettily you've grown! Your hair and eyes are much darker than they used to be."

"I think fair hair often darkens," I said.

"And of course your poor father was dark. It was your mother, God rest her, who had the golden hair. Perhaps it's as well as you don't favour her. Less painful all round."

I had no idea what she was talking about, so I smiled and let it pass. It was now clear to me that she'd been a servant at Lucy House and knew you very well when you were a child, so I decided to tread warily in case I stirred suspicion in her mind.

We went down to the back parlour where there was a plentiful meal laid out for the two of us. "You'll not mind our eating together, Miss Anne?" she enquired anxiously. "We often used to in the old days."

"I shall be glad of the company," I said truthfully. While I ate she would probably talk and make it easier for me to be you! However she said very little, and nothing of the days before you came to the academy. I kept reminding myself that you also have no recollection of them, so I was not really lying when I pleaded forgetfulness.

Incidentally, has it never struck you as odd that you recall scarcely anything of your childhood? I can remember my own years in the orphanage most vividly. The matron was a good woman and did her best for all the inmates and, though there were no luxuries and few pleasures, nothing very dreadful happened to me there that, in later life, I would choose to forget.

She talked a little about Yorkshire. "A wild, bleak place with terrible winter weather that freezes you to the marrow of your bones! I can tell you, Miss Anne, that I suffered cruel from the ague when I was first there, but after a while a body gets accustomed. The people round about are a mite clannish—not that West Country folk are different! You'll know how we look upon anyone from north of the Tamar as a foreigner! But they're good-hearted under their rough tongues."

"Lord Sinclair—my uncle?" I ventured.

"He's a good man, respected." There was a sudden constraint in her voice. "He has two mills over in York, and then he does a deal of charity work too, but he's not an easy man to know. He'll do his duty by you, though, and see you brought out in society. And looking at you, Miss Anne, I reckon it won't be long before there are suitors rapping at the door."

(Dear Anne, I hope you will not think it vain in me to repeat such compliments. You have always insisted to me that I am pretty, and I would be a hypocrite to look in my glass and deny it. What I lack are your intellect and your accomplishments.)

When she spoke of suitors, I experienced a flutter of pleasure. At that moment I could almost have persuaded myself that it will be possible for me to marry a lord. However, I am not completely indifferent to reality. For the next three months, I will enjoy a taste of the luxury that is your destiny and, at the same time, while avoiding any engagement that would have to be broken when my true identity is revealed, I will most certainly look about me for a clergyman or a squire who would not be too embarrassed to take a wife from the lower classes.

"Tell me about Sinclair House," I invited.

"Oh, it's a grand big house," she said with enthusiasm, "much larger than Lucy House. It's not in York itself but about ten miles outside the city on the edge of Rombalds Moor. There are several large estates round there and a lot of comings and goings between the young people of the households, so you'll not lack for friends."

"My uncle said that Lady Tatlock will act as my chaperone?"

"So I've been told." Again there was constraint in her voice. "She's a widowed lady who has houses in London and York. She's staying in York this summer, and she's acquainted with all the right people. She dresses very elegant."

"And my uncle? What is he like?" I asked, adding hastily, "I only recall seeing him once."

(Odd to reflect that I was actually speaking the truth. I had glimpsed him crossing the hall at the academy, his cloak wrapped around a little girl with fair hair. I did not then know who he was, of course, and the next morning Miss Turnbull told me there was a new pupil, and I was to show her round and make her feel at home.)

"Lord Sinclair is a good man," Dorcas said. "As a master he's hard but fair. I think you will have to form your own opinions, Miss Anne, when you've known him for a little while."

That didn't sound too promising, but I reminded myself that it would only be for a couple of months anyway before you returned from France and confessed our scheme. I hoped that once he had recovered from the initial shock, he would regard it as an excellent jest at his expense. I am writing that with hindsight in the past tense because, though I have been here for only a few days, I have learned that Buckfast Sinclair is not a man to take any sort of jest with equanimity.

But I am running ahead of myself! Dorcas and I finished our meal, by which time it was quite late. I confess that I would have liked to see something of the city by night, but I had enough sense not to shock Dorcas by suggesting it. Instead I yawned and complained the journey had fatigued me, which was not untrue, and we went up to the bedchamber. She is clearly suspicious of city ways for, although the door had an inner bolt, she also tilted a chair beneath the door handle so that, I assume, the noise made by an intruder would waken us. But intruders were as scarce as footpads, and I slept soundly until dawn!

We boarded the coach just after six. Dorcas took charge, seeing to the loading of the baggage, insisting loudly that we had paid for two window seats. She is a managing, good-hearted sort of woman, and I was glad to have her there.

I had no more than a glimpse of the tall buildings

and the spires of the city before we were bowling northward out of London. The city seemed to continue on into narrow streets and rows of tiny houses, and then we were in open country again. It was a fine, warm day, and, once one had become accustomed to the jolting of the coach, the journey was very pleasant. However, one cannot spend an entire day staring wordlessly through a window, and I soon began to study my fellow passengers.

There were two ladies, sisters I was given to understand, who were travelling to Wakefield to attend their niece's wedding. They talked a great deal about the young lady and the splendid catch she had made until I grew quite weary of hearing about her.

"The second cousin of an earl's younger brother is not to be sneezed at!" one of them exclaimed.

"Why, only eight people stand between him and the earldom," the other announced.

A rather pale young gentleman, who sat in the corner opposite my own remarked gravely, "We must certainly pray for plague this summer, or perhaps a shooting party might be arranged to lend colour to the honeymoon."

"Well, really! We had scarcely begun to think along those lines!" one of the ladies began.

"My dear ma'am, one should take a practical view," the gentleman said. "Now plague might be a difficult matter to arrange, but there are endless possibilities in a shooting party. Indeed I have many relatives whom I would like to invite to such a function."

I gaped at him as did everyone else in the coach, for he looked so serious, and then I spotted the twinkle lurking at the back of his eyes and was forced to bite my lips heartily to avoid giggling. Opposite me Dorcas gave a loud sniff, though I am not certain if it was designed to convey her opinion of people who boasted of their high connections or those who advocated killing off their relatives.

The two ladies lapsed into an offended and puzzled silence, and a stout gentleman who had apparently been dozing straightened up and began to give us all advice on how to run the government.

"For now that the talk concerning Princess Charlotte's condition is proved to be premature there is a dearth of acceptable royal heirs. The Royal Marriages Act should be repealed, so that the dukes may wed sensible women and infuse new blood into the Hanoverian line. We don't want another mad monarch!"

"A sane one would be an agreeable novelty," the young man said, and this time I could not refrain from a smothered chuckle, which I hastily turned into a cough.

"For my own part," said one of the wedding guest ladies, "I do not believe it can ever be morally correct for anyone to gossip about one's betters."

"Yet one could scarcely be blamed for excluding the Princess of Wales from that category," her sister remarked. "I hear her latest excapades are quite scandalous—not that one wishes to pass judgement without knowing all the facts!"

"I do hope you will not allow such a trifling consideration to deter you," the young man begged.

After that, the affairs of the royal family were freely aired by everybody except Dorcas and me. She maintained an unbending silence, and I was too occupied with keeping a straight face and avoiding the mischievous glances cast at me by the incorrigible young gentleman in the corner. Lest you fancy I have already fallen in love, my dear Anne, let me quickly assure you that the said gentleman and I did not exchange one word of conversation, even when we paused for re-freshments at the posting inns, and, after he left the coach at Doncaster, I had quite forgotten what he looked like within five minutes.

The wedding guest ladies left us at Wakefield. I believe that we all looked out to see if they were met by the second cousin of the earl's young half-brother, but there was nobody there to meet them more impos-ing than a rather elderly looking coachman.

By this time, I had grown weary of sitting in a stuffy coach. Had I been a servant, I might have joined in the general gossip, but, being a young lady, I was forced to maintain a discreet silence! The sun had long since begun to drop behind the horizon, and the landscape had become very wild and bleak, with great swathes of moorland and rock at each side of the highway. One really might have fancied oneself back on Dartmoor. It had also become somewhat colder. Those of us left in the coach began to wrap ourselves more tightly in shawls and cloaks, and the stout gentleman wound a muffler several times about his neck.

By the time we saw the walls and arched gateways of York, I was thoroughly fatigued and hoped very much that our journey was almost done. Dorcas had said that Sinclair House was about ten miles outside the city, but, for all I knew, they may have been country miles.

"Adam is come to meet us," Dorcas said as we rattled into a large posting yard, and our driver blew a long blast on his horn to announce our safe arrival.

I must confess that my heart sank as I climbed stiffly down to the cobbles and beheld a carriage with a crest upon the doors drawn up at the side and a dour visaged individual at the horses' heads. I would have liked to stretch my legs and take a hot drink, but the man stepped forward, greeted us with a brusque nod, and proceeded to give directions for my luggage to be transferred to the other vehicle.

"Tha mun wrap up warm," he instructed us both as he held open the door. " 'Tis reet parky."

I assumed he meant cold, for quite apart from the circumstances of his using an unfamiliar word, he spoke in an accent that was difficult for my ear to follow. They nearly all, save Dorcas, speak thus round here, which adds to the sense of isolation, though I suppose it would not do for me to be chattering to the servants all the time!

We entered the coach and having had no more than a glimpse of the outskirts of the city, were off again, the horses bounding forward as if they scented their stable. We left the main highway after a mile or so and turned into a narrower track that followed the convolutions of the landscape, now rising to bleak, wind-swept rock, now falling into peat-black valley with a stream rushing through. I could see the twisted branches of trees against the skyline and here and there the lights of some homestead gleaming through the swift gathering dark.

"I reckon your uncle will find you as changed as I did, Miss Anne," Dorcas remarked.

I trusted silently that he would not find me so greatly changed that he denounced me as the imposter I am, but, of course, I could not say so to her. Instead I said, "Tell me something of the household. Are there many servants kept?"

"There's Adam and the two grooms and a couple of women who help with the rough work, but they don't sleep within the walls," she told me. "There's Peter who is footman and Arthur—Mr. Arthur I should say—who is butler and valet both and Cook and Rosie and Martha who are parlourmaids and two lassies from the orphan asylum who work belowstairs."

It was the mention of an orphan asylum that made me sit up a little more erect, determined that whatever happened I would play my part—*your* part—to the best of my ability. Nobody would guess for one instant that what education I have has been gathered up in between dusting Miss Turnbull's china cabinet and clearing away the dishes. I would be a real young lady for one summer and trust that when you returned from France the consequences would not be too serious. Perhaps by then I will have met the second cousin of an earl's younger half-brother!

It was quite dark by the time we reached a pair of high iron gates that stood open, with an avenue of elm trees leading to another arched gateway lit by two lamps that swung in the wind as we drove between them. We drew up in a courtyard with walls at left and right and, opposite the gate, a large stonebuilt house with many chimneys and lights burning in the windows.

"We will soon have you warm and comfortable, Miss Anne," Dorcas said in a tone that patted me on the shoulder and told me not to fret.

Adam came to open the coach door and, at the other side of the yard, I saw another manservant standing with a lantern held aloft.

"Is that Mistress Grant?" the man called.

"Who else would it be?" she retorted tartly. "I'm back with Miss Anne, of course."

"Happen we thought tha'd stayed in London and run off with Prinny," he said.

"I might have done if the Regent had laid eyes on

me," Dorcas said chuckling. "Make your bow to Miss Anne, Peter, for she's been travelling these two days and is both tired and hungry!"

"Miss Anne." Peter gave an awkward sort of a bow. "T'maister's says you've t'go right to him. He's waiting."

I had expected some leisure in which to freshen myself before being presented to Buckfast Sinclair, and I must have drawn back instinctively because Dorcas said quickly, "Miss Anne will be there directly, Peter. We'll take off our cloaks first."

I felt her hand on my arm, urging me into a square, stone-flagged hall and then up a narrow wooden staircase and along a panelled corridor to a handsomely appointed bedchamber. There was fire burning in a large fireplace, and candles were lit, imparting a mellow glow to the figured velvet hangings.

"I swore death and destruction if all wasn't made ready," Dorcas said, looking round critically. From the way she spoke, I surmised that she filled the post of housekeeper here.

I took off my cloak and changed my travelling shoes for a pair of lighter slippers. It is fortunate that you and I can even wear the same gloves and shoes, is it not? I wish that I had had time to put another dress on, for the blue one needed brushing and the lace yoke was limp, but I smoothed it down, and Dorcas, obviously trying to conceal her anxiety, fussed around, winding my curls about her fingers and giving me a damp cloth to remove the traces of dust from my face.

"You'd better go down to your uncle, Miss Anne," she said. "He'll have held back supper on your account, and he's a gentleman doesn't like to be kept waiting."

I swallowed nervously and she looked at me kindly,

"The dining room is at the left of the main entrance," she told me. "We came in through the side door."

"Then I'll go down." I gave her a questioning look, and she opened the door and directed me through an archway to a gallery that overlooked a large hall with two handsome chandeliers lighting up walls hung with woven cloth and stained glass windows between. There was a very fine red and gold patterned carpet on the stairs and the floor below. As I went down, I could feel my heart fluttering like a canary in a cage, and I am sure my colour had fled.

The dining room door was open. I had a confused impression of rich and sombre luxury, and then a tall gentleman turned from the high mantel where he stood staring down into the leaping flames.

Anne, you never told me that your uncle is still quite young. Perhaps you had forgotten. He is certainly short of forty, though there is about him that habit of authority which makes a man look older. He is powerfully built with harshly marked features and dark hair and eyes, and his voice is brusque.

"Come in, come in! There is no need to stand on ceremony," he said, as I lifted my hand to tap on the door panel.

I went in and bobbed a little curtsey. "I am happy to see you again, uncle," I said.

"So now we have dispensed with the formalities," he said, "we can sit down and eat. I take it you had a comfortable journey."

"A tiring one."

"After supper, you must feel free to seek repose. Dorcas had been tending to the preparations for your arrival, so, if you have any complaints, make them to her."

"I am not the complaining type," I said mildly.

"If that is true then you differ from every female of my acquaintance," he remarked and gestured to a high backed chair at the end of a table that would have comfortably seated twelve. He took the chair at the other end, and we gazed at each other for a moment or two across an expanse of white damask.

"Do you find me greatly altered?" I ventured.

"It would be surprising if you were not, as you were only ten years old when we met before," he answered. "At that time I had so much business to attend that I had scant opportunity to pay much heed to you."

"When my papa died and you took me to the Turnbull Academy."

"You remember that? Do you recall anything else?"

I shook my head.

"It's as well," he said surprisingly, but though I looked a question he didn't elaborate.

The man called Peter came in with an older man whom I assumed correctly to be Mr. Arthur. They both began to serve the meal, which was much better than anything we'd ever eaten at school. I was halfway through the roast partridge when I realized that he was frowning down the table at me.

"I said that you have not yet touched your wine. Do you want something else?"

"We didn't have wine at school." I picked up my glass hastily and sipped the ruby red liquid.

"You are not at school now and must learn to take your place in the adult world," he said, "but if you prefer to drink lemonade—"

"The wine," I said hastily, "is fine," and took a mouthful.

"There is no need," he said unsmilingly, "to force yourself into accepting what you may find unpleasant. Maturity brings with it the freedom of choice."

"Oh," I said weakly and took another sip. I would have liked to enquire what freedom of choice had been given to his niece, but I deemed it wiser to remain silent.

The partridges were followed by a selection of cheeses and some very fine dessert pears. I was engaged in peeling mine when he said abruptly, "You will require fashionable gowns. I am no judge of sartorial elegance, but the dress you are wearing will scarcely do for the Assembly Rooms at York."

"You said that Lady Tatlock—" I began.

"Lady Cora Tatlock has kindly offered to accompany you to her dressmaker's in order to purchase whatever is needful for your wardrobe, and she will act as your chaperone when the occasion demands it. She is a lady of impeccable taste and has been most kind in her offer of help."

I don't why it is, but, when I am informed that someone has impeccable taste and the kindest of intentions, I prepare to dislike them. I made some indeterminate murmur in reply, however, and finished peeling the pear.

"I usually take coffee in the drawing room," he said. "You will join me there?"

It was a request couched in a tone that required an affirmative answer. I gave it, and, the pear eaten, followed him into another large, handsomely furnished room where a silver coffee service held pride of place on a table between two upright armchairs. I poured out two cups and handed one to him.

"This is a very fine chamber," I said, more to break the silence than anything else.

"I bought the house when I came up into Yorkshire, and saw to its redecoration and furnishing," he told me. "I have lived here now for nearly seventeen years and am not likely to move. It is near enough to the city to enable me to keep my business affairs running smoothly but not hemmed in by other houses. The grounds here are quite extensive."

"I shall enjoy exploring them," I said.

"There is not much for a young person to do." He sent the frowning look towards me again. "Your reports from school were very good. I read them with some interest. Miss Turnbull regards you as a pupil of some considerable academic promise."

"I am sure that she exaggerated," I said quickly. "I can speak French quite well, and my needlework is good, but I am not near as clever as she may have led you to believe."

"Well, cleverness is not a requisite in a wife," he observed. "I doubt if the lack of it will stand in the way of your obtaining a husband."

I drank my coffee, trusting that he would believe the flush on my cheeks was due to the heat of the liquid. In truth, I was beginning to feel a little irritated at the calm, cold manner in which he summed me up and outlined my future without once enquiring my opinion.

"I hope freedom of choice extends to the acceptance of a husband," I said at last.

"Naturally you are free to choose." He raised his thick eyebrows. "It is not my intention to wed you by force to one of those black-hearted villians who crop up in those novels all the ladies appear to be reading these days."

"One does not take such tales for reality," I said defensively.

"Does one not?" He gave me a slight smile and looked suddenly much younger.

"Of course not," I said. "Real life is far more exciting and romantic than anything in a book."

The smile had vanished, and the look he gave me was a brooding one. "If that is all you have derived from your schooling," he said curtly, "then Miss Turnbull does, indeed, appear to have exaggerated your intelligence. However, it is the fashion for people to talk nonsense these days, I'm told. I seldom go into society and so cannot tell."

Anne, you judged him rightly when you told me that his letter revealed him to be both arrogant and uncouth. He makes it so clear that I am nothing but a tiresome burden to be disposed of in matrimony as speedily as possible. Yet, he has clearly taken some thought for my comfort in sending Dorcas, whom, I suppose, he expected me to remember, and in arranging for this Lady Cora Tatlock to launch me in the polite world.

I finished my coffee and asked if I might be excused, as by this time my eyelids were drooping. He rose as I rose, bidding me goodnight in a civil if not a cordial way. I bobbed a curtsey and hoped that he was not expecting any warmer demonstration. It seemed he was not, but he suddenly took a pace nearer and stared at me most intently, so intently that I felt a flutter of apprehension.

Then he said, almost as if he were speaking to himself, "No, you do not resemble her. You do not resemble her at all." He made an abrupt sawing gesture with his hand and, returning to the hearth, stared down into the flames.

I went into the hall and up the staircase to the bedroom where Dorcas had unpacked, and the covers were turned down.

I have more to tell you, my dear Anne, but it must wait until I have more leisure.

Your loving friend,
Anna.

= 2 =

MY DEAR ANNE,

This is really a continuation of my last letter, which I have not yet sent. That first evening at Sinclair House set the pattern for what is clearly to be the tone of the relationship between Buckfast Sinclair and myself. We meet for supper, which is at seven sharp, and, seated at each end of that long table, make desultory conversation until it is time to rise and go into the drawing room, where I pour the coffee. Then, when we have exchanged a few more sentences, I bid him good night and go upstairs. He treats me with a kind of bored courtesy which is only one degree removed from rudeness, and I am sure he will be delighted when I am launched upon the matrimonial market, and he can wash his hands of me.

This is a magnificent house and a lovely estate, with gardens and woodland set like an oasis in an expanse of heather-clad moor. I suppose that unless Lord Sinclair marries, the property will come to you. It is very wrong of me to feel envy, but I do, for by then you will have made an advantageous marriage and have a home of your own. Perhaps if I do not catch a clergyman, you will allow me to be housekeeper here. I begin to fear that, once this deception is revealed, nobody again will ever make any effort to employ me!

There are ten bedchambers and, apart from the servants' quarters and kitchen, six large reception rooms, including a library crammed with books, a charming parlour, and a long room at the back of the house where it would be possible to hold a modest ball for six to eight couples. Everything is so luxuriously appointed that it is obvious your grandfather must have been a very rich man.

From what you yourself told me and from the odd remark tossed out by Dorcas, I have gleaned that when your grandfather died, he divided his property between his sons. John, the elder, who was your papa, also inherited the title. He moved to Devon, and Buckfast, the younger, came into Yorkshire, though the Sinclairs were a Hampshire family of Norman descent. There is a shield among the trophies in the billiards room that carries the name St. Clair and is supposed to be very ancient. How odd it seems to be telling you about your own family!

One fact I have already discovered. On the second—no, the third evening after my arrival here—I was drinking the obligatory cup of coffee, and I remarked on the lack of family portraits. Your—*my* uncle looked up with the faint frown between his brows that I have come to recognise. "I was not on the best of terms with my relatives, so there is no reason why I should be forced to look at them day after day," he said curtly.

"Not even with your—my papa?" I said.

"John was four years my senior, and, even as boys, we were never close," he said. "After Father died, we went our separate ways."

"And when papa was killed, that was the first time you came to Lucy House?"

"It was my duty to make the necessary arrangements for the funeral and to settle you in a suitable female establishment. Lucy House has been rented out together with the surrounding farmland."

"Is it profitable?" (It was really none of my business to ask such a question, but I was curious.)

"The estate brings in an income of five thousand pounds a year, of which, now that you are eighteen and subject to my approval, you have use of the interest. That has accrued during the past eight years to approximately fifteen thousand pounds. There are various running expenses that have to be deducted, but when you have a mind to see the books, I can show everything to you."

"Oh, there is no necessity." I felt suddenly embarrassed. "I never had a head for figures."

"Your marks in arithmetic have been consistently high."

"Only in comparison," I said vaguely. "Fifteen thousand pounds seems like a deal of money. Papa must have left a considerable estate."

"As you say." He frowned again, glancing towards the clock. I took that as a hint that he was weary of my company and, a few minutes later, took my leave and retired.

My days were, at first, spent in exploring the house and grounds. He, my uncle, went out early ever morning. "He makes it his business to oversee the estate and take a personal interest in the mills," Dorcas told me. "He speaks in the Lords, too, when he's down in London, on the emancipation of the slaves and not having children under the age of seven working."

It occurred to me that we might have stayed at his

town house instead of at an inn when we broke our journey up to Yorkshire, but, when I mentioned it, she shook her head.

"The house is closed up for all the year save for a suite of bachelor chambers your uncle uses when he is in the city. I suppose the entire house will be opened up when you go down to start your London season proper."

(But of course that will be you, my dear Anne, and not myself. I only trust, now that I have gauged his upright, unbending temper, that he will still give you a London season when he learns the truth.)

"He works very hard for a man who is rich enough not to have to work," I commented.

"Different folk have different ways of forgetting," Dorcas said. I would have gone on to ask her what he was trying to forget, though I believe that I am beginning to guess. I'll not venture to write it down yet until I am certain. Dorcas had quitted the room before I could continue the conversation, and I was left to amuse myself as best as I could. I put on my cloak and went for a walk in the grounds. The gardens are planted in sheltered hollows with high hedges to keep out the blustering winds, and many of the plants are grown under glass, which further protects them from the icy winters here.

I do not relish long walks as you have always done, but I did stray a considerable distance from the house, until I began to walk up the grassy slope that led to the rim of the moors beyond. Those moors have their own loveliness, not orderly and exquisite like the gardens, but wild and fugitive. The sun will suddenly emerge and bathe the grey lichen that clings to the rocks in a flood of gold, or one may see a splash of harebells dancing in an unexpected wind where, a moment before, there was only clumped thistle and dark swathes of peat.

I stood looking over the landscape, and saw a horseman riding up the slope. For a moment, with the sun in my eyes, I saw only the dark figure against the horizon, and then the thudding hooves slowed and stopped, and Buckfast Sinclair reined in his mount and stared down at me.

"Is anything amiss?" he enquired sharply.

"I was taking a walk," I said.

"A marathon, more like!" He sounded amused. "I did not realise athletics were taught at the Turnbull Academy!"

"Oh, ladies do have legs that work, uncle," I said demurely. "It is merely that we do not often use them."

"Even so, you ought not to wander so far by yourself," he remarked.

"The moors are so beautiful."

"They are seen to their best advantage from the saddle." He swung his leg over and dismounted. "I will give you a ride home."

"I cannot ride," I confessed. "Riding was not on the curriculum at the academy."

"But as a child you rode well. Mistress Dorcas told me once that you were absolutely fearless."

"I have not ridden since—since papa was killed," I said.

"I will pick out a quiet filly and give you some instruction myself. That art once learned is never forgotten."

"I have no riding habit."

"That is an item of your wardrobe that will be attended to very shortly."

He had looped the reins over his arm and was

walking by my side. As we entered the wood, the leaves cast flickering shadows over his face.

"Chosen by Lady Tatlock?"

"Guided by her. Naturally she will consult your own preferences."

"This wardrobe?" I said hesitatingly. "It is to come out of my income, I assume."

"Then your assumption is wrong." His voice was cold. "I am not yet so miserly that I will not buy my niece what is necessary for her coming out."

I dared not protest further, but I began to experience decided pangs of guilt. The clothes made for me, though they will fit you when the time comes for me to hand them over, may not be in the right colours. Your complexion is rosier than mine, your hair fair, and your eyes almost grey. The shades that suit me will be too vivid for you. I comforted myself with the reflection that young girls generally wear paler colours anyway, and we walked on towards the house.

"Tomorrow, I shall take you into York," he said. "Be ready at nine o'clock. Lady Cora is devoting the entire day to you."

I did not much relish being treated as if I were a charity case, but I again made the murmuring response that might have been mistaken for gratitude, and, a few moments later, we separated, he going towards the stables, myself entering the house, where I went into the parlour and amused myself by leafing through some sketches.

The next morning, I came out punctually at nine to find the crested coach waiting with Adam on the driving seat and milord standing on the step. He gave a swift apprizing look at my grey pelisse and my straw bonnet, and I could tell that he thought my clothes were dowdy, but I reasoned that he could scarcely expect me to appear like a fashion plate before I had received the benefit of Lady Tatlock's advice.

He handed me in and took his seat beside me as we rolled down the drive. I feared that our drive to York might be a silent one, but he began to point out various landmarks that I had not clearly discerned on the evening I had travelled towards Sinclair House.

"That is Shuck Hound Hill. It has the rough outline of a dog's head with its ears pricked."

"Why 'shuck hound'?" I asked.

"There are legends that the shuck hound appears to warn of impending doom. It has a black coat and red eyes that glow like coals in the dark."

"Have you ever seen it?"

"Only those who believe in it see it," he said.

"Then I shall take care never to believe in it," I promised him, and he laughed. Such a light, easy, pleasant sound that took all the brooding from his face.

"What's that?" I gestured through the window towards a building that looked like a summerhouse, save that its roof was gone and ivy grew thickly about its pillars.

"That's False Lass Folly."

"And is there a legend about it?" I asked, encouragingly.

"A local squire loved a girl and built the folly as a place where she could sit in the shade on a hot day. She used to come out here with her groom to watch the progress of its building."

"And?" I said as he paused.

"She eloped with the groom before the roof was put on, and the squire left it as it was as a souvenir of female inconstancy."

"Because of one girl?" I exclaimed.

"See one, see all," he answered, with a sudden down

curve to his lips that made me change the subject hastily and enquire where Lady Tatlock lived.

"She has taken a house near Clifford's Tower," he told me. "I understand the dressmaker and the milliner will both be there. You will spend the day choosing patterns and being measured and fitted, while I take refuge in my club. I am promised that the gowns, bonnets, and other fripperies will be ready in two weeks, so you may rest content in the knowledge that you have provided employment for a regiment of sewing maids."

I thought of you then, Anne, and wondered how you were progressing at the Chateau Lanuit and if you had wearied of the novelty of being a servant. And I knew, quite suddenly, that I was enjoying being a fine lady, even if my presence was not entirely welcome. It will be hard for me to return to what I was before.

We passed by a round tower built on a green mound and drove down a long street with handsome houses at each side, stopping before one of them.

"Lady Cora will be a tremendous help to you," my companion said as he helped me down to the pavement. "She is experienced in the ways of society and knows exactly how things should be done."

Someone must have noted our arrival. I saw the twitch of a lace curtain at an upper window and, as we mounted the front steps, a footman opened the door and ushered us in.

"My dear Buckfast, how splendid that you are come!"

A lady came down a flight of stairs towards us. Floated, rather than walked, with emerald green chiffon billowing about her like a cloud of leaves.

I had expected Lady Tatlock to be middle-aged, but this lady was scarce thirty, with auburn curls cut short above her ears and a voluptuous figure revealed rather than concealed by her draperies.

"Good-morning, Cora." He kissed the hand she held out to him.

"Morning? La! 'tis the middle of the night!" she protested. "It will take me several more weeks before I am accustomed again to country hours."

"I am sure you will adapt. You are one of the most adaptable women I know," he said.

"How horrid of you to make me sound exactly like a chameleon," she pouted. "You will take a cup of chocolate with me as penance?"

"It would be pleasure, not penance," he said at once, "but it is not possible today."

"Meaning you will drink champagne and eat kidney pie at your club. And this is your niece?"

"My manners always desert me when I am in the presence of beauty," he said with a gallantry so unlike his usual manner that I gaped at him.

"Anne, this is Lady Cora Tatlock. Cora, my niece."

"But she is truly exquisite! I declare that if she were not your niece I would be jealous!" she exclaimed. "She looks so grown-up for eighteen."

I thought, as I curtsied, that was hardly surprising since I am twenty-two.

"And surely you mentioned fair hair?" She was looking at me rather more attentively than was comfortable.

"My hair used to be lighter when I was a child," I said.

"It is still a very pretty brown—so much more subtle than blonde," she said. "You have a very taking figure too! Very charming indeed! Now you have promised me a free hand, Buckfast. We shall startle the ton with our protegée."

"I beg you will not be too startling," he returned laughing. "She is fresh from the schoolroom."

"And will tempt jaded palates," she returned. "Go away, Buckfast, and return at six. We will take an early supper together."

She had grasped my hand and was hurrying me up the stairs. We entered what was clearly the main reception room, which was so crammed with bolts of material, bonnets, boxes of gloves, shoes, and trimmings, that it looked like chaos come again. In the middle of it all stood two women clad in black with pins stuck in their bodices and tape measures round their necks.

"This is Miss Sinclair, who is shortly to come out," Lady Cora announced. "She is to be fitted with everything she requires, and one gown must be ready for this evening."

Anne, I must tell you that being measured and fitted for clothes is the most exhausting pastime, but one also derives tremendous pleasure from it.

I am to have three ball gowns—the absolute minimum for a first season, I was assured. One is of spotted white muslin under a peplum of strawberry pink, with a feathered headband to match; another is of blue and white, with sprays of pale pink rosebuds looping up the hem, and the third is a very soft orange, with trimmings of white and pale green. I am to have three evening capes to blend with all these shades, a frogged riding habit with a skirt that ends above my ankles, some dresses for morning calls in silk and muslin, two pelisses, of which one is in mole grey velvet, half a dozen bonnets—my mouth watered as patterns were chosen and trimmings discussed.

Buckfast Sinclair had been right in his estimation of Lady Cora as a woman of taste. Certainly she has an unerring eye for colour and a sensuous delight in finely woven fabrics. I stood for hours while I was measured, draped, and pinned by one of the dressmakers, while the other sat in a corner and stitched rapidly at a dress that Lady Cora had declared must be ready for me to wear by the time my uncle returned.

"It is in the cutting of a garment that a dressmaker displays her art," Lady Cora said. "Simplicity is actually most subtle and complicated. Had I not been born into my present station in life, I would have become a dressmaker, I believe."

I could tell that she truly did believe it, but I could not avoid thinking that it was very easy for a rich society lady to cherish ambitions that would never have to be realised.

We broke off at noon for a nuncheon that we took at a small table in an adjoining room. It was served to us by a correct, unbending footman whom Lady Cora addressed as James.

"Not that it is his baptismal name, my dear, but it is so much less fatiguing to call all the footmen James and all the parlour maids Molly."

"Why not just give them numbers, ma'am?" I suggested.

"La! What a droll idea!" She tinkled a laugh at me. "One can see that you are destined to be an original, my dear Anne! Wit in a woman is like the rum in a pudding—a little adds piquancy but too much gives one the most appalling headache. How do you enjoy life at Sinclair House? For my own part, I would find it too terribly remote, but I am a social butterfly—or so Buckfast tells me."

"He said you were a very dear friend."

"Heavens! how dull that makes me sound, as if I were already fat and forty." She made a rueful little face. "Of course, one does generally expect widows to be so, which is grossly unfair on those of us who are not yet ready to leap into the grave after our late lamented spouses! Come, let us return to our task. I had a quantity of gloves and slippers delivered for you to try."

Tiring as it was, it was also most stimulating. I daresay that you, having always been of a more serious turn of mind than myself, would have found it all very tedious, but I have always adored pretty things, and the prospect of being admired was delightful.

For all her affirmations that she would have liked to be a dressmaker, Lady Cora chattered away as freely as if the two women in the room were stone-deaf and had no feelings or opinions of their own. It was evident that she did not consider them to be real people at all. She told me a great deal about her friends, who were all, according to her, gay and amusing people. It seemed that anyone who was not gay and amusing stood no chance of advancement in society, so I privately resolved to be both.

"Not that dear Buckfast is particularly light of heart," she informed me. "I tease him that he will become a crusty old bachelor if someone does not take him in hand. Yet, he can be the most charming of men."

I had seen him being charming to her and felt a twinge of irritation that he could not exert himself to be particularly charming to me. But then Lady Cora was a sophisticated woman of the world, and I was only his niece, for whom he had no particular affection but by whom he was resolved to do the correct thing.

"We must dress you in the new gown," she said at last. "Of course, it is very simple and modest, but it will give Buckfast some idea of what to expect when the other garments are ready."

The dress was round necked and short sleeved, in a

very pale rose silk, with a long velvet ribbon in a deeper rose at the high waistline. A pair of ivory slippers and gloves were pronounced to be suitable accessories, and then Lady Cora summoned her maid, who came to comb my hair into tighter ringlets and secure them with pink ribbons.

"You do not need rouge or powder," Lady Cora said.

I fancied there was a trace of wistfulness in her tone, but it was gone directly as she said, "Now we will go downstairs and wait for your uncle to arrive. Fortunately, he is always punctual, for, if there is one thing I cannot endure, it is to be kept waiting, especially by a gentleman."

We went into a room where there was a love seat and several stools covered with embroidered black velvet and an oval gilt mirror before which she prinked for a few moments. Certainly, she is an attractive woman, her attraction stemming more from vivacity of expression than regularity of feature.

It was not many moments before we heard the doorbell ring, and then my uncle—for so I must think of him—came in and Lady Cora cried, "Do you not think she looks delightful? I am prodigiously pleased with the results."

"They justify the effort," was all he said, but his dark eyes rested on me with an expression warmer than any I had yet seen.

"She must return for final fittings in about ten days," Lady Cora said. "And within the next week the garments will be ready, and the launching may proceed."

She spoke as if I were a ship about to slip down into the ocean where it would either sink to the bottom immediately or sail triumphantly into warmer climes.

"It will commence in a fairly modest manner,"

Buckfast said, as we went through into a small dining room. "I have to entertain the local clergy and their wives to a tea party in a fortnight."

"The clergy!" She raised her plucked eyebrows as we took our seats. "How too terribly dull for you!"

"I have the bestowal of several livings, two of which have recently fallen vacant," he explained. "Anne can act as my hostess."

"You do not think my presence as chaperone—"

"At a ball or a rout, of course, but I cannot imagine she will be in any great danger among the cloth."

"You must wear the blue morning dress with the long sleeves," Lady Cora said to me. "Clergymen always like the colour blue—it puts them in mind of the heavens, I suppose. And it will not be necessary for you to be brilliant. Clergymen are too accustomed to talking themselves to listen to anyone else, and their wives will be too overawed by their surroundings to pay any heed to what is said."

"Cora, you are incorrigible! I would not dare let you loose on a flock of clergymen," he said, looking immensely amused.

The footman whose name wasn't really James served us with duck terrine and thin fingers of toast. I noticed that Lady Cora nibbled at her portion with a preoccupied air as if she was not terribly interested in what was on her plate. Evidently, hearty appetites are not fashionable, so I curbed my own with some difficulty and pushed morsels into my mouth with an air of doing so entirely by accident, while my uncle and our hostess talked about mutual acquaintances of whom I had never heard.

"The Glenvilles are returning," she said. "Their elder son would be quite a feather in Anne's cap. He is heir to the baronetcy, you know."

"And was sent down from Oxford for belonging to a Mohawk Society."

"Five years since, and the Mohawks are quite out of fashion now!"

"I am sorry that vandalism and roughness should ever have been *in* fashion," he remarked. "But one cannot hold youthful follies against a man for ever, I suppose. Perhaps Robert has improved."

"Not that there is any great hurry to make a match," Lady Cora said. She had darted a quick glance at me and was evidently aware of my private discomfiture.

"The season proper will not begin until the autumn. One may regard this as a trial run, so to speak. It would be unwise to enter into any precipitate engagement before the presentation at Court."

"Knowing the royal appetites, it might provide some measure of safety," he remarked.

"Nonsense, the Prince Regent only ever falls in love with older women. Your niece will be far too young to draw the royal attention," she assured him.

"Then the Regent is not the arbiter of taste we all imagine," he said. "Anne looks exceedingly pretty."

"This is a mere prelude to how she will look when all her gowns are completed," Lady Cora declared. "She has a very pretty wit also to spice her looks. If her accomplishments match, then she will have a brilliant season at the end of which you will be giving her away at the altar."

"Let us not leap our fences before we have ridden the course," he answered. There was a slight irritable note in his voice, but then chicken with walnut dressing and a tureen of new peas were brought in, and he began to talk about the improvement in culinary standards since the French Revolution.

"So many cooks lost their situations in aristocratic

households and had to flee that other countries have reaped the benefit. I am fortunate in that my cook, though she is Yorkshire born and bred, spent some months working for an emigré family and is a very light hand with sauces."

The conversation had shifted from my chances of catching a husband to the more comfortable trivialities of everyday living. I was glad of it, for I know very well that I will never actually make my curtsey to the Prince Regent or attend a London ball. The best for which I can hope is to snare a clergyman, so I must remember to be very charming indeed when they descend on us for tea!

When we had eaten the lemon meringue that succeeded the chicken, my uncle rose, saying that he had instructed Adam to bring the carriage round before seven-thirty.

"Which means you will abandon me to a solitary evening," she pouted.

"On the day you are condemned to spend an evening alone, my dear Cora, I will resign my seat in the Lord's and take up ditch-digging," he retorted. "I am certain that at least half a dozen people will have called upon you before the clock strikes ten."

"Unhappily they are not always the people one wishes to see," she answered.

"In a week or ten days then?" He kissed her hand. "I truly appreciate your help in this matter."

"Oh, I shall expect ample return for the favour." She spoke archly, smiling up into his face.

I guessed then that she had decided to take another husband and had marked down her quarry. I wondered if he too was aware of it and if he would allow himself to be chased and caught.

"Thank you, Lady Cora." I spoke with genuine

gratitude, for whatever her motives, she had shown me great kindness. Her maid servant brought a parcel in which were the clothes in which I had arrived, and I went out to the carriage with my uncle.

Twilight was falling, and, after the warm house, the air felt chill on my bare arms. As we drove off, I could not repress a small shiver, and he glanced at me sharply.

"Have you no shawl?"

"My pelisse is in there." I indicated the parcel.

"You had better wrap yourself in this." He was untying the laces of his heavy cape. "By the time you have struggled with the knots, you will have caught your death of cold."

"Which would be a great waste of all those new clothes," I jested.

"A waste of more than that." He put the cloak about me, pulling it close. "You have a very bright future ahead of you, my dear."

"As wife to Robert—whatever his name is?"

"Glenville. The Glenvilles are well enough, but it is my hope that you will do better than that."

"I would like to marry where I love," I ventured.

"Love does not exist save in the imaginations of romantic young ladies," he said lightly. "And, if it does exist, then it is as fleeting as snow in April. One glimpses its sparkle, and then the rains come."

"And the flowers grow," I said obstinately.

"Also the weeds! Remember False Lass Folly!" He gave me his downcurving smile in which there was more of remembered pain than pleasure.

I snuggled deeper into his cloak, shaking my head a little, and smiling as if to assure him that I was determined to hold onto my romantic notions. The cloak was warm and heavy, like two arms holding me closely. We rode in silence the rest of the way, and, when we rattled over the cobbles of the stableyard, I felt for the first time as if I were coming home.

Dorcas was waiting to exclaim over the new gown, and I slipped off the cloak and gave it back to its owner. As he had already eaten, there was no reason for us to be together, and he did not seek my company.

I look forward to seeing Lady Cora again. She would make him a splendid wife, for I am certain that she does not believe in the permanence of love either, and her antecedents are doubtless impeccable. And my own opportunity may come at the tea party of the clergy. There is bound to be an unmarried one among them.

I do not believe I will post this to you; at least not until I have some small social triumph to report.

My love to you,
Anna.

— 3 —

Sinclair House,
Yorkshire.
Thursday.

MY DEAR ANNE,

It is nearly three weeks since I took pen in hand to write to you. As I have not yet sent the letters, I suppose that it is foolish of me to have a conscience about not continuing to write, but I was always a mite illogical.

I have spent two more days in York, though my uncle did not accompany me. Instead, Adam drove me and delivered me, and though Lady Cora's greeting was friendly, I sensed that she was disappointed I had arrived alone. Nevertheless, we had a congenial day. The dresses were all nearly completed, save for the final touches, and it was vastly entertaining to dress myself in one ensemble after another while the two women tweaked at bows and pulled at ruffles and debated the merits of a fringed parasol over a scalloped edge one. The clothes are all so charming and, as if I were in a play, when I am wearing them, I feel myself to be more and more the Honourable Miss Anne Sinclair and less and less plain Anna Sayle.

Lady Cora and I arranged that I would return after three days when everything would be quite ready, and I did return to be greeted by boxes and parcels in which all my finery was packed.

"Save for this morning dress," Lady Cora said. "We will take a little drive through the town when you have changed into it and allow the good citizens a peep. I am quite excited at the prospect of the stir your looks will cause."

It is an odd trait in human nature, I suppose, to wish to be praised for what we are not, but I couldn't help wishing that I possessed your own acute mind and independent spirit. Buckfast Sinclair is not a man to be content merely with a pretty face.

She had a very smart rig waiting when we descended the staircase, with one of the Jameses standing up behind in the tiger's place while she herself took the reins in a capable manner than belied her fragile air.

York is a very beautiful place, immensely ancient, as one can see from the walls that surround it and the turreted gateways, but it is also bustling and fashionable, with some delightful shops and a number of coffee houses where it is de rigueur for gentlemen to discuss business.

"Though I suspect most of them complain about their wives," Lady Cora said. "I know my own frequently did."

"Surely not, ma'am!"

"Surely yes!" she returned, laughing. "Poor dear Frederick wished only to be left alone with his collection of stamps and coins and could not endure being dragged out to parties. However, he was always very good-humoured about it, though I am certain he unburdened himself to his friends on the sad trials of having a flibbertigibbet wife. Ah! there are the Harris girls. Not much competition for you there! Beatrice is in her third season and has landed nobody, and Celia is woefully shy."

"Perhaps they have not yet fallen in love," I said.

"Love?" She pronounced the word as if it were an

unfamiliar one, into whose meaning she would have to enquire. "We are talking of making a good match, my dear, though naturally one expects to be fond of one's husband."

"Naturally," I said and thought to myself that I would expect to feel a much stronger emotion than that before I agreed to marry anyone.

We stopped before a small restaurant, where Lady Cora announced we would drink a cup of tea and eat a macaroon.

"Not that a lady alone would enter a public eating place unescorted, but for two ladies to take some refreshment together is eminently correct. Afterwards, we will drive back slowly. It is such a pity that Margaret Townsend is not yet in York. She knows everybody worth knowing and is a most amusing companion, but I understand she stayed at Buxton to take the waters. We will meet her in London, and if she takes a fancy to you, then you may set your cap at a duke and very likely snare him!"

Several ladies stopped at our table to exchange greetings with Lady Cora. To all of them she introduced me as "Miss Anne Sinclair, Lord Sinclair's niece and ward. She is on the threshold of her first season."

It conjured up a vision of me about to be pushed into the middle of a crowded room full of young ladies armed with spears with which they intended to pin down the hapless young gentlemen seated around the walls! The thought of that amused me so much that I wanted to tell Lady Cora, but thought better of it. She is a good humoured woman, but she regards the social scene as a very grave matter indeed. I do wonder what she would say if she learned there is not the least possibility of my catching a titled gentleman, though I might get a younger son!

All the ladies smiled and bowed and looked me over, while I sipped my tea and nibbled at a macaroon. Then we re-entered our vehicle and drove back to her house, where we found Lord Sinclair waiting.

"I completed my business sooner than I expected and am come to escort my niece home," he explained.

"And I cannot prevail upon you to stay for supper?" She pouted a little, her head tilted.

"Not even for afternoon tea, of which I am sure you have both partaken," he returned.

"Then you may go home, and I will remain solitary and forlorn."

"My dear Cora, I am convinced that you will not remain so for longer than the time it takes you to change your gown," he said smilingly.

"You have not forgotten that you promised to escort me to the Assembly Rooms on Tuesday?"

"I have not forgotten." He took her hand and drew it to his lips, and I suddenly felt cross and fidgety for no reason at all.

When we were in the carriage, he looked at me and remarked, "So you have run the gauntlet of the mamma's! Did you find it a sad ordeal?"

"It was amusing," I informed him. "All the ladies who have daughters of their own pierced me through their lorgnettes, and those who have sons were charming. I imagine every mother would like to bring an heiress into the family."

"And some are quite blatant about it," he agreed laughing. "In your case, however, I am sure it is not merely the thought of the money that will please them. You do look extremely charming."

"I hope to do you credit when the season starts," I said.

"Anne, you must not get the notion into your head

that you are obligated to me in any way." The amusement had fled from his face, and his voice was cool. "Since your father's death, I have performed no more than my duty in seeing the estate was profitably run and in seeing that you received a good education. When you have met a gentleman who makes an offer you feel able to accept then my responsibility is at an end."

"Then I will make haste to accept an eligible gentleman and relieve you of the burden," I said lightly.

"It was not intended to sound quite like that," he said frowning.

I gave him what I hoped was a cool self-possessed little smile and turned my head to look through the window. We were passing False Lass Folly, and I remembered the story and felt angry that the girl would always be remembered as false, when it was likely she had loved her groom and been true to him.

A few days later—the day before yesterday, in fact—the clergymen came to tea. It being a fine day, the long windows at the back of the house were opened and some cane chairs set out. A long table was piled with cakes, pies, and sandwiches, and there were several smaller tables at which the guests could sit. It gave a pleasantly informal touch to the proceedings.

I had dressed with some care. This might be my opportunity to attract the regard of a young, unmarried minister who would be happy to take me when the truth emerged. At the same time, I had to remember I was Lord Sinclair's niece and, for the moment at least, destined for a more brilliant marriage. My new gown of spotted white muslin with a sash of sapphire blue and a fichu of delicate lace was, I hoped, exactly suited to the occasion. I wound my hair into a demure chignon, and my straw bonnet was tied with a blue ribbon.

Dorcas, who came to inform me the first arrivals were just turning in at the gate, was very complimentary.

"You look beautiful, Miss Anne, far too good for a parcel of clergymen! You know I would never have believed you'd turn out so lovely. You were such a plain little scrap, all eyes and chin! And now you look like a princess. Nobody would know you for the same person!"

"If the visitors are here, I had better go down," I interrupted. "Is my uncle there?"

"Oh, Lord Sinclair may not like these affairs, but he always attends," she told me. "Your being here to do the honours will be a great help to him."

I went down and was barely in time to reach his side before they began to troop in. I had expected to be a trifle nervous, for it was the first time I had ever acted as hostess, but he made it easy for me, shaking hands, his voice and manner cordial as he greeted them and introduced me.

There must have been about thirty clergymen, most of them with their wives, a few with their daughters. It struck me that many of the latter were probably hoping to catch a clergyman, too, and lead him to the altar.

"Mr. Brontë, I am delighted to see you again." My uncle was shaking hands with a tall red-haired man. "My niece, Anne Sinclair. She has just completed her schooling in Devon. Mrs. Brontë comes from the West Country, Anne."

"From Penzance." The plain little lady at Mr. Brontë's side spoke in a soft Cornish accent.

"I have never been into Cornwall," I said. "I am told parts of it are very wild and picturesque."

"But the winters are mild. In Penzance, we have flowers all the year round." There was a faintly wistful note in her voice.

"The northern climate is more bracing," her husband said in a strong Irish accent.

"Mr. Brontë holds the living at Thornton. Am I right in saying you recently had an addition to your family?" my uncle said.

"A little girl, Charlotte, born in April," Mrs. Brontë nodded.

"Our third daughter. Maria is two and Elizabeth just over a year. We are hoping for a son next time. My wife was reluctant to leave them even for a few hours, but my wife's sister is staying with us and has taken charge. An occasional foray into congenial company is beneficial, is it not? Ah!" Mr. Brontë stopped speaking for a moment to beckon toward a young man. "I hope you Lordship will not take it amiss, but I took the liberty of bringing a friend. Mr. Joshua Knight is the son of a former compatriot of mine now settled in Essex, where I began my own ministry. He hopes to find a living in Yorkshire."

It was the pale-faced young gentleman from the coach. I recognised those twinkling green eyes and was surprised to discover they belonged to a minister.

"Miss Sinclair and I are already acquainted," he said, shaking hands. "We were both on the same stage travelling up from London, though we did not exchange any conversation."

"Then we had best remedy the lack," I said brightly. "I am very glad to see you again, Mr. Knight."

Most people had drifted towards the long table and were helping themselves to the refreshments. Lord

Sinclair had escorted the diminutive Mrs. Brontë to one of the smaller tables and was helping her to a cup of tea and some scones. The room was full of black coats and gaiters and ladies in print gowns and bonnets slightly out of fashion.

"Let us get some tea and sit in the open air," Mr. Knight said at my elbow.

"When everybody is served and settled." I smiled at him and moved away to carry out my duties as hostess.

"I will hold you to that." He smiled back and went to take his turn in the group around the capacious teapot.

Seeing him again was like seeing an old friend. I went about my task of ensuring everybody had what they required with a light step, and at the end of ten minutes found Mr. Knight at my heels again.

"Come and drink your tea before it is completely stewed," he invited.

I allowed him to lead me to one of the tables outside, where I sat while he took the chair opposite.

"This seems like fate, does it not? I trust you are as delighted to see me as I am to see you," he remarked.

"Surely that's not for a lady to admit," I said, and he chuckled.

"Ah! we are now bound by conventions instead of being flung pell-mell into a rattling coach! But I claim the privilege of an old friend."

"On what grounds?"

"On the grounds that we both know the relatives of the second cousin of an earl's half-brother."

"I do hope the ladies enjoyed the wedding."

"And were handsomely regaled at the reception, though I doubt if they would enjoy such a lavish spread as has been provided here today."

"My uncle says that clergymen eat a very great deal—oh! I beg your pardon!" My face had crimsoned with embarrassment as I realized my tongue was running away with me.

"Your uncle is absolutely right," he said solemnly. "I intend to preach a sermon on gluttony the first opportunity I get."

"You have a living?"

"Assistant to my father at the moment. I hope to obtain a curacy here in the north."

I wondered if he was being attentive to me in the hope of obtaining one of the two livings my uncle held in his gift, but it was plain that his admiration was genuine.

"I wish you good fortune, Mr. Knight." I raised my teacup slightly. "Are you staying with Mr. and Mrs. Brontë?"

"I have taken temporary lodgings nearby as Mrs. Brontë, in my opinion, has more than enough to do with looking after the children."

"That was considerate of you," I said.

"Oh, I am not quite a saint." He looked amused. "I will confess to you privately that I am very fond of children, but not when three of them are all crying at once!"

"But you like it here in Yorkshire?"

"I like it more now," he said.

"Did they teach you to pay compliments in theological college?"

"Paying compliments comes naturally to me when the lady is beautiful."

"I can see that you are going to be very dangerous clergyman, Mr. Knight—were one tempted to take you seriously!"

"Anne!" Lord Sinclair had approached. "I am sure

Mr. Knight will excuse you, but the Jeffersons wish to hear something about the Turnbull Academy. They have a daughter who is going to school as soon as a suitable one has been chosen."

"Excuse me." I finished my tea and went over to where the Jeffersons sat. I had been recalled somewhat abruptly to my duties as hostess, but perhaps Lord Sinclair had heard some of the conversation and considered it risqué.

The tea party lasted for nearly two hours and was far less of an ordeal than I had feared. I told the Jeffersons all about Miss Turnbull's establishment, making it sound, of course, as if I had been a pupil there. I circulated in the approved manner, pressing more cake and sandwiches upon people, smiling sweetly, conscious of Joshua Knight's green eyes following me.

There was one odd little occurrence which I will relate.

I had gone over to speak to the Brontës for a few moments, and Mrs. Brontë remarked, "Of course, if you were reared in the West Country, then you will require to wrap up very warmly when the winter comes, but it must be very pleasant to be with your uncle in such a lovely house after being reared at school with no family."

"Only for eight years, ma'am. Before that I was at Lucy House." I began, but she broke in, her voice surprised.

"Lucy House! But wasn't that where—?"

"On the borders of Devon and Cornwall," her husband said. "Is that not right, Miss Sinclair?"

"Yes. You've heard of the estate?" I asked the question of Mrs. Brontë, but she shook her head, crumbling the bit of cake on her plate.

"There are so many fine old properties in the West Country," she said vaguely. "Tintagel is a very great favourite of mine. The scenery round about is quite magnificent."

I am certain she had started out to say something else and then changed her mind, but there was no time to steer the conversation back again, for Mr. Brontë had begun to talk of his native Ireland and of the ancient castles there, and, shortly after that, as if some invisible bell had rung, the clerical visitors rose and took their departure en masse.

I found Joshua Knight at my side.

"I am driving back with the Brontës to Thornton. We hired a carriage, as they don't keep one, but I intend to buy a horse and take some excursions over the moors."

"You will combine your search for a curacy with some pleasure, then?"

"I hope the pleasure will include taking tea with you again." He held my hand longer than was strictly necessary as he shook it.

"The clergy are always welcome in this house," I said and dropped a mocking little curtsey that made him chuckle.

(Written down, it sounds rather trivial and foolish, but I have had so little fun in my life that I enjoyed our banter, and there was a certain excitement in having a young man treat me with such flirtatious friendliness.)

I said good-bye to the last of them as they went sobersuited down the drive and then went upstairs to take off my bonnet. The sun had shone brilliantly all the afternoon, and, when I went downstairs again, the gardens were bathed in a rosy glow. This is such a beautiful place. There are moments when I wish I might stay here!

"So! Next year they will clutter up one of my neighbours' lawns!" Buckfast Sinclair had come towards me from the direction of the stables. He looked so vastly relieved to have them gone that I could not help exclaiming,

"Surely, you did not find it such a burden! You treated them with such courtesy."

"I was hardly likely to inform them that I found them all a confounded nuisance," he said. "Oh, they are well enough, I suppose, but I like to keep Sinclair House inviolate from intrusion. However, I have two or three possibles for the living, but I will consult with the bishop before I make a final choice."

"Mr. Knight hopes for a Yorkshire curacy," I said.

"Mr. Knight has his eyes on a great deal more." He glanced obliquely at me as we re-entered the house. "Actually he comes of good stock, an old Anglo-Irish family. His father was a younger son and settled in Essex. There is some money there but not an enormous amount. It gives the young man ambitions."

"There is nothing wrong with ambition," I said.

"Not if it is directed aright. He seemed mightily interested in you!"

"We travelled together on the stage," I reminded him.

"And on the strength of that he claims a lifelong friendship."

"I hope," I said, "that you will not allow his partiality for me to prejudice you when it comes to making a decision."

"Then you admit he has a partiality!" He gave me another frowning glance. "Well, one can scarcely blame him. You both looked and behaved charmingly—only I'd not want my niece to come out of school and fall head over heels for a clergyman!"

"Oh, I am aware that I am destined for a duke!" I said flippantly.

"I wish you to be happy, Anne." He spoke with a sudden and disarming gentleness. "It is not given to many of us to be happy, but for you I wish it. I'd not have you leap into some rash entanglement that would cause you pain nor have you accept an offer not to your liking in the mistaken belief that you were pleasing me. You are going to be a rich young lady, and the husband you choose must match you."

"Perhaps I will choose not to wed at all," I said. "Perhaps I will reject all offers and go to live at Lucy House."

"You do remember it then?"

I shook my head truthfully. "Little Mrs. Brontë said that she had heard of it. She seemed on the point of saying more, but the conversation took another turn," I told him.

"So." He frowned, then gave a slight shrug as if he were working out some problem in his own mind and had reached a not altogether satisfying decision. "So, when the time comes, I am sure you will make the right choice."

He mounted the staircase to his own quarters, while I, watching from below, reflected that, when the time of decision came, I would not be the one who would return or not to Lucy House.

That evening he had ridden out to keep an engagement, when I went into the dining room, and I dined in solitary state with the place opposite me vacant.

Yesterday, when I came down into the main hall, he called to me from the library. He was in breeches and riding coat and looked handsome. When he is not frowning or withdrawing behind an impenetrable wall of chilly politeness, he does look really quite handsome.

"It is time you took up riding again," he said, and my heart sank into my slippers. I was not even sure if I liked horses. Certainly, I have never in my life had riding lessons.

"I'm really not sure," I began, but he cut me short with genial impatience.

"Nonsense! Dorcas tells me that you used to be a fearless little rider. The shock of your father's accident ought not to ruin your enjoyment for the rest of your life. Run upstairs and put on your habit while I wait."

There was absolutely nothing to be done but comply. I went as slowly as I could and took as long a time as I dared to change into the calf-length skirt and frogged jacket and high boots, but dressing cannot be prolonged for ever. When I descended the staircase again my uncle was pacing the hall.

"You took longer than most women take to dress for a ball!" he exclaimed. "I've a filly with a sweet temper that will suit you very well, for she's sure-footed as well as swift."

There was no way of avoiding what lay ahead. In a few moments, I would be thrust up to the back of a strange animal with no more notion of how to ride it than how to fly. We walked across the dew damp lawn in the direction of the stables with me lagging a few steps behind.

"You really are nervous!" He had paused at the arch that led to the stable and turned to give me a sweeping glance. "I promise you there is no cause! The manner in which my brother rode was always reckless. He was fortunate not to break his neck sooner. You and I will take things more slowly, I promise you."

"It might be best," I said, "if we pretended I had never ridden before and you were giving me my first lessons."

"If you wish, though riding is like walking. Once learned, it is never forgotten."

He put his arm about my shoulders as we went into the yard. There was the smell of hay and sweat and leather, and a couple of grooms touched their forelocks.

"You keep a lot of horses!" I said foolishly.

"I breed and race them. Had you forgotten that, too?"

"I wasn't aware of it," I murmured, and jumped nervously as a high pitched whinny sounded from a nearby stall.

"That's Jasper!" my uncle said, moving away from me. "He knows my voice and my step. Not this morning, boy! This morning we're taking out the ladies. Anne, come and meet Gemini."

"Why Gemini?"

"Out of Castor and Pollux," he answered.

"Who were they?" I asked.

"Two bright stars that cannot be distinguished— surely you've heard of them!"

"Oh, I don't think we ever did very much about astronomy at school," I said hastily. "So this is Gemini. She's very pretty."

She was also much larger than I expected. I looked up at her somewhat apprehensively.

"Give her this." My uncle took an apple from his pocket. "She adores russets—On the flat of your palm! You cannot have forgotten every mortal thing!"

I advanced my hand within snapping distance, closing my eyes briefly, but the filly took the apple daintily and crunched it up.

"Tom! Bring a lady's saddle for Miss Anne!" My uncle, turning, had commanded one of the grooms.

I stepped back as the lad came with the halter and, opening the lower half of the door, led the animal out.

"Put her on a leading rein. It's several years since my niece was in the saddle," my uncle said.

We went out into the yard again. There was a mounting block there. I tried desperately to recall from which side I had seen other people mount up, but my mind was a blank.

"Come, come! there is no need to be so nervous," my uncle said. "Easy!"

"Nor any need for you to address me as if I were a horse myself," I said, and found myself laughing. And then, without knowing quite how I got there, I was in the saddle with my leg hooked in the approved manner and the reins in my hands. The cobblestones seemed a very long way below me, but my uncle took the leading rein and walked Gemini, with me on her back, under the archway into the gardens.

"Relax your muscles," he ordered me. "There is no need to cling on so tightly. We are going to take a gentle walk until your confidence returns."

I refrained from telling him that I'd not had any confidence in the first place and tried to relax. In fact, as I became accustomed to the motion, I began to enjoy the sensation. I even began to hope that in a short time I would be trotting and cantering at my own pace.

"You are certainly out of practice," he remarked, shattering my dream. "However, if you ride every morning for half an hour, there'll be a vast improvement in a short space. When I am not here, Adam will instruct you. He has forgotten more about horseflesh than I ever knew."

"And Gemini is sweet-tempered."

"She is a real lady." He stroked her velvety nose, and she nuzzled her head against his shoulder as if she were whispering secrets.

"And faithful?" I said.

"Completely—but then she is horse, not woman. Enough for today! You will be as stiff as a poker if you remain aloft."

He turned to help me dismount, and, an instant later, his arms were about me, and my feet were on solid ground again. When I looked up, he was looking down at me with a little pucker between his brows. Then he spoke briskly, putting me at arms length.

"For a first lesson that would have been promising had you been a complete novice. It's obvious that you need a lot of practice before you can regain your skill. Walk Gemini back to the stables, and help the groom to unsaddle her. Make her accustomed to the sound of your voice and the touch of your hands."

"Did my mother ride?" I heard myself say. I cannot imagine what prompted me to ask the question, but I knew at once it had been an error.

A shutter closed firmly behind his face, and he said coldly, "Well enough. The important thing is to get your own riding up to a reasonable standard as quickly as possible." He walked off with no further word and left me staring after him.

This morning, when I came down, Adam had brought Gemini round to the steps. There was no sign of Lord Sinclair, who had gone off "on business" when I returned from the stables after that first lesson. He did not return for dinner, and he has still not returned as I write this.

Probably he stayed over in York, possibly spent the

evening with Lady Cora, who, I am sure, will be an excellent horsewoman.

Anyway it really is, as I keep reminding myself, none of my concern.

Your affectionate friend,
Anna.

—4—

Sinclair House.
Wednesday.

MY DEAR ANNE,

I have been thinking about you a great deal these last few days. It is strange to be living in your world, looking at people and events through my own eyes. What is even stranger to me is that I have settled into this world so well. I had expected to be far more nervous and clumsy, but, apart from having to guard my tongue to a certain extent, I feel very much at my ease.

The fact that I have apparently altered since I was a child was noted and accepted without question. I have discovered that people see what they expect to see and accept one for what one claims to be. Miss Anne Sinclair was due to arrive in Yorkshire, and it has never entered anyone's head that a serving maid who spent her childhood in an orphanage might be here instead. I don't suppose anyone has asked you if you are an heiress in disguise, though I am certain you are regarded as a very superior sewing maid!

In this two weeks since I last wrote a great deal has happened, and so I will endeavor to put everything in the right order. First, then, I must tell you that I have ridden every day and am making excellent progress. Thank heavens I seem to have a naturally good seat in the saddle, and Lord Sinclair tells me that I will soon regain all my former daring! Yes, he has accompanied me, riding his stallion, Jasper, and I have achieved a trotting pace, but not yet a canter! We ride for up to an hour every morning, leaving the gardens and taking the bridle path through the woods until we reach the crest of the moors. They are in all their summer loveliness now, great swathes of purple heather and golden broom sweeping to a grey-green horizon, and the sun turning the little brooks to silver.

"They must be magnificent when they change colour in the autumn!" I exclaimed on one such occasion.

"By then, you will be in London, astonishing the ton with your beauty and wit," Lord Sinclair said.

"Will you open up your town house?" I asked.

"Lady Cora and I discussed that," he said. "It will make much better sense if you stay with her, since you are making your debut under her auspices."

"But won't you be there?" I asked.

"I shall probably put in the occasional appearance, to make sure my niece is enjoying herself," he said.

"But you will escort me surely?"

"My dear, when you reach London," he said, "there will be a regiment of young gentlemen longing to escort you. You'll have no time for a mere uncle."

I opened my mouth to argue further and suddenly realised my own foolishness. When the time comes for the Honourable Miss Anne Sinclair to dazzle London with her beauty, it will be you who will dazzle them. By then, I will have caught my clergyman. Indeed, I suspect that I have already caught him, but I am running ahead of myself as usual!

I have not yet reached the standard of horsemanship when I can ride out alone, but I do walk in the gardens and the wood often alone. You know, at school I was neither a full pupil nor a full servant, but balanced between the two. You were the only real friend I made, and I fell into the habit, when you were not there, of going apart from the rest. Perhaps I have been trying to discover who I truly am, deep inside myself, and what I want out of life, and the habit has remained with me.

So I spend part of each day simply walking, and, as I walk, I pretend that I am truly a rich young lady and have every right to live in this beautiful house and walk in these gardens. It is, I tell myself, a harmless fantasy.

I was walking there a few days after the clergy had been entertained to tea, when I saw a rider trotting up the bridle path and stood aside as he neared me and reined in his mount.

"It has to be Miss Sinclair!" he exclaimed.

"Yes, but I don't—"

"Glenville. Robert Glenville." He swung himself clear of the saddle and held out his hand. "I was told the loveliest girl in England was come into Yorkshire, so I came ahead of my family to find out for myself if it was true."

"And is it?" I accepted his handshake.

"It is not true," he said. "You are clearly the most beautiful girl in Europe."

"Why not the world?" I said, laughing. "Why stop at Europe?"

"Oh, one ought not to exaggerate," he said. "It is barely possible that in some remote corner of an as yet unexplored continent there is a young lady who surpasses you."

"You are talking a deal of nonsense." I tried to sound severe as I withdrew my hand, but the corners of my mouth quirked. He was a handsome young gentleman with curling brown hair and a reckless face.

"Not one syllable!" he protested, looping the reins over his arm and falling into step beside me. "I assure you I never talk nonsense where pretty ladies are concerned. A friend of my mama's saw you in York and said you were quite exquisite."

"I would have been with Lady Tatlock, I suppose."

"With Lady Cora, yes. You are coming out in society, under her auspices?"

"She has been very kind."

"Of course she has! Lady Cora hopes to change her second name to Sinclair, and she regards her chaperonage of you as a step nearer her goal. Oh, there is no need to look so disapproving. The whole of Yorkshire is talking about the pursuit and laying bets on the outcome."

"Then it is a pity," I said, "that the whole of Yorkshire does not have something more worthwhile to occupy its time!"

"There is not much else to talk about since Boney was exiled," he said, not one jot abashed by my indignation. "For my part, I think the chances are even. Lady Cora is as determined to be wed again as your uncle is to escape the snare of matrimony. Of course, he may succumb to her blandishments now that he is getting on in years."

"My uncle is not yet forty," I said coldly.

We had left the wood and entered the garden. The house basked in the sunshine, all the window panes glittering like sharp points of diamanté.

"My mama's age," Robert Glenville said and nodded at me.

"Then she must have been married before she was out of the schoolroom," I countered.

"How she would love you if you told her that!" he exclaimed. "Actually, mama has been on the verge of forty for some five or six years now."

"You ought to display more respect," I scolded.

"Respect is going out of fashion. Had you not heard? Will you make your debut at the Assembly Rooms in the next few days? There is to be a ball on Monday."

"I don't know yet what plans have been made," I said.

"If you are there, will you save me three dances?" he asked.

"Perhaps we had better wait until I know what plans have been made," I said firmly.

"Ah! you are as cautious as your uncle!" he exclaimed. "I hoped you would take after Wild Jack."

"Who?"

"Wild—" He hesitated, sudden embarrassment in his lively face. "Oh, it was just a name some people gave to your father when he was a young man."

I wanted to ask more, but he held out his hand again. "You are about to invite me in to take some refreshment, but I cannot stay. I've a pressing engagement in York that will not keep. I could not, however, resist riding this way in the hope of seeing the estimable Miss Anne Sinclair."

"And now you have seen her."

"Indeed I have and she is—incomparable! Come to the ball, Miss Sinclair. Without you, the Assembly Rooms will be a desert!"

He was riding away before I could frame a retort. I stood looking after him, amused and a little bewildered by the brief encounter.

When I sat down to table that night Lord Sinclair remarked, "So you had a visitor?"

"Dorcas has sharp eyes," I said, a little nettled. "As a matter of fact, Robert Glenville called."

"Glenville is a young puppy in need of curbing," he remarked.

"Because he paid his respects? Surely there was no harm in that!"

"The young man has a bad reputation. He was sent down from the university and since then wastes his time in gaming halls and at the cockfight."

"Perhaps he needs a wife to settle him down," I suggested.

"It is my hope that you will find a partner more worthy."

"I am not likely to find any partner at all while I remain secluded here," I said. "I have been in the neighbourhood for some weeks now; my wardrobe is complete—and all I have done is drink tea with Lady Cora and hand round sandwiches to the clergy."

"You are bored here?" His voice and expression showed disappointment.

"You misunderstand me!" I said swiftly. "I am happy here. I have never been so happy! But I know that I must marry, and I cannot choose or be chosen while I am secluded."

"Cora has put forth the same argument." He frowned slightly. "As you say, you ought to begin to go out and about a little. There is a ball at the Assembly Rooms on Monday. I will inform her that she may begin her duties as chaperone in earnest."

"Thank you, uncle!"

My face glowed, but he cut short my thanks with an upraised hand. "Going to the ball does not imply approval of Robert Glenville. He is a wild young man with no sense of responsibility."

"Like Wild Jack?" I said.

"What? Where did you hear that phrase?" he said sharply. "I told Dorcas. . . . Then you are beginning to remember? I hoped that you would not."

"I am not sure," I said cautiously, "how much there is to remember."

"My elder brother was a man of great charm and very few principles," he said curtly. "Wild Jack Sinclair had a reputation that grieved our father deeply. The title passed to him, together with half the family fortune, and, in his will, our father expressed the hope that we would each use our share wisely. I came up into Yorkshire. Jack went to Devon and proceeded to fill his house with riff-raff. You have heard of the Mohawks and the Hell Fire Club?"

"Very vaguely. They were not topics of general conversation at school."

"They were societies comprised of rich, idle, vicious young men who thought it great sport to indulge in blasphemy and drunkeness and other vices. My brother drew his friends from those ranks. I heard reports when I was in London and wrote to remonstrate, but he told me—with some justice, I must admit—that he had no intention of taking orders from a younger brother. Then news came of his death in a riding accident. I went down to Devon at once to make the funeral arrangements. The estate had been mismanaged, and you, yourself, alternately spoilt and neglected. You were very shocked and bewildered, so I judged it best to put you immediately into more congenial circumstances."

"But you did not bring me back to Yorkshire with you."

"I was still a young man, not yet thirty, with no wife. I thought it would be better to put you into a school where there would be other children."

"You never wrote or visited."

"I did what I considered to be right." He looked at me stonily. "I have avoided personal involvement. It brings too many complications."

"You must have hated your brother very much," I said.

"Hated?" He shook his head. "That isn't quite the right word. I used to think there was nobody in the world like Jack when we were boys. He was four years older than I was, four years ahead of me in everything. I used to admire everything he did, until I grew old enough to realise that most of what he did was not a matter for admiration. I saw the effect of his conduct on our parents. My mother defended him to the last, but when she died, about a year before father, she admitted how much he had hurt her. Anne, this cannot be pleasant for you to hear. I think it would be better if we dropped the subject."

"It does not upset me. I find it interesting," I said incautiously.

"Interesting!" he echoed. "We are, after all, talking about your father."

I wanted to tell him that we were not. We were talking about my friend's father, and so nothing I might hear could affect me personally.

But I could not, of course, say that. Instead, I said cautiously, "I am no longer a bewildered child. What you tell me makes me more grateful to you for the care you've taken of my welfare."

"Grateful." He repeated the word, his mouth wry. "I am not sure if gratitude is not a two-edged weapon. I have done no more than duty commanded. Now eat your dinner, or you will lack the stamina for an evening in the Assembly Rooms."

Which meant I would be attending the ball. I felt anticipation rise up in me. Oh, for the people who went regularly out and about in society it would not be a special occasion, but for me, who has been nowhere, it holds all the promise of a magic I once believed would be forever out of my reach.

"It would not be fitting for you to stay from the beginning to the end, since you are not yet officially presented," my uncle told me. "I will accompany Lady Cora and yourself to the event at nine o'clock, and we will leave directly after supper."

I must have looked disappointed because he added with a teasing note, "A taste is often more enjoyable than an entire feast. You will soon grow weary of attending routs and balls."

I thought that in the highest degree unlikely, but held my peace. For whatever length of time I was permitted to remain, I intended to enjoy myself thoroughly. I was so glad that Miss Turnbull had permitted me to attend some of the dancing lessons that Miss Jennifer gave. I never could understand why you found them so tedious.

I wore the blue spotted muslin gown. It is so pretty, with the neckline cut low and the sleeves tiny puffs, and the skirt caught up at the hem and ruched with sprays of pale pink rosebuds. Dorcas dressed my hair for me, catching the back up into a ring of rosebuds, fluffing the ringlets out around my temples.

"You'll be the belle of the ball, Miss Anne," she informed me. "There'll not be another one there to hold a candle to you!" I smiled at her as she helped me put on my long cape with its blue lining and collar of white fur. I am not so foolish that I believe literally everything she says, but I knew this was going to be a very special evening, untouched by reality.

When I went downstairs, Lord Sinclair was waiting for me. He looked splendid in full evening dress, with his cravat tied just so, his cloak swinging from his broad shoulders, his white gloves in his hand. I felt a thrill of pleasure at the realization that I would enter the Assembly Rooms on the arm of such a distinguished-looking escort, and my pleasure was only slightly dimmed by the knowledge that Lady Cora would be at his other side.

"You will do me credit," was all he said, but there was a look in his dark eyes that made me feel suddenly shy. In a moment, I would begin to babble like a fool.

We entered the coach and bowled down the drive. The last of the daylight was beginning to fade. When we returned, it would be past midnight and completely dark.

Lady Cora emerged from her front door just as we drew up outside her house, so our arrival had been waited for. She had on a very beautiful dress of lavender and green against which her red hair glowed, and there were emeralds at her throat and in her ears. Yet, as she settled herself in the coach, I could not help noticing the lines around her mouth and eyes. She was probably a few years past thirty and denying it to herself. I chided myself for the uncharitable thought and gave her my warmest smile.

"Here is your card, dear, and pencil." She looped them about my wrist. "You will have time for two, possibly three dances. It depends on how speedily the master of ceremonies can form the sets. I hope you have eaten a little something. At supper, one merely nibbles. I assume you can make shift to dance the polka and the gavotte? There were dancing lessons given at that academy?"

"Yes, ma'am, but there were no gentlemen. We danced with one another."

"Remember you will be dancing with male partners tonight, and do not be tempted to take the lead. It is a pity you are not staying for the entire evening, but, under the circumstances, to arrive late and depart early is eminently correct. I understand that young Glenville has already paid his addresses."

"A brief call," I said.

"Then you may depend upon it that he will be there, though the rest of his family has not yet arrived.

Don't allow him more than one dance. Do not allow anyone more than one dance."

"It would be difficult to do otherwise, ma'am, if I am only to be there for a short space of time," I said as we drew up before a lighted building from which music was issuing.

I thought to myself, "This is me, Anne Sayle of nowhere in particular, transformed into Miss Anne Sinclair of Sinclair House, and I am going to my first ball—whatever happens in my life from now on I will always hold the memory of this."

Then I was stepping from the coach and going up the steps into a brightly lit foyer, beyond which I could see arches and a shallower flight of stairs. An attendant took my cloak, and another preceded us to the head of the stairs, waiting until the last few bars of music had died away.

"Lady Cora Tatlock. Lord Buckfast Sinclair and the Honourable Miss Anne Sinclair."

The master of ceremonies was making the announcement as the three of us went down into a glittering chaos of polished floor, a row of cane and gilt chairs, long curtains looped back with velvet bows, a forest of eyes turned in our direction.

"There are not so many here tonight," Lady Cora murmured in a disappointed tone.

I gave her an astonished look, for it seemed to me that we were surrounded by people. And the girls were all so pretty in their delicate silks, low-heeled slippers tapping beneath the hems of their skirts, fans raised to hide their mouths as they turned to whisper.

"Miss Sinclair, it is delightful to see you here."

I had expected to see Robert Glenville, but I had not expected to see Joshua Knight, who was bowing before us, his green eyes twinkling.

"Mr. Knight! I had no idea you were in York." I shook hands with pleasure. "I had no idea clergymen came to such occasions."

"Oh, the Church places no ban upon dancing," he said lightly. "I have one or two interviews in York, so am staying here for a few days."

"Lady Cora, may I introduce Mr. Knight? Lady Cora Tatlock. Mr. Knight is staying with the Brontës at Thornton. My uncle you already know."

"Are the Brontës anybody?" Lady Cora said in an aside.

"Nobody at all, ma'am." Catching the remark, he sent her a sorrowful look. "If one does not think of them, they simply cease to exist!"

"Miss Sinclair, I was about to lay a wager on your putting us in the depths of despair by not coming!" Robert Glenville had reached us. "I am happy I did not, since I would have lost my money, quite apart from the severe disappointment I would have suffered. The next dance is to be a gavotte—"

"Which I am about to beg Miss Sinclair to partner me in," Joshua Knight interposed.

"I believe Miss Sinclair will tell you that she is already engaged to stand up with me," Robert Glenville began.

"I claim benefit of clergy," said Joshua Knight.

"Gentlemen, my niece will naturally open the ball with me," Lord Sinclair said.

"Buckfast, you never dance!" Lady Cora exclaimed.

"Tonight, I dance." There was a glint in his eyes. "Come along, Anne. They are beginning to form the sets. Gentlemen, I am sure that Lady Tatlock will be charitable enough to partner one of you."

"You extricated me from an awkward situation," I said.

"Which you apparently leapt into of your own accord in the first place. What possessed you to go making rash promises?"

"He assumed I had," I said.

"You had better learn to be rather less lavish with your smiles in future," he said. "Two admirers glaring at each other will attract attention."

"Perhaps they will fight a duel," I said and chuckled at the idea.

"If it were not that such an incident would ruin your reputation, I'd offer to act as second for the pair of them," he answered, his lips twitching.

"Do you really never dance?" I asked curiously as the measure began. "You seem to be very light on your feet."

"You may change your opinion when I come down heavily on your toe," he warned. "I escort Lady Cora frequently, but I am considerate enough to leave her toes unbruised."

"But with me you are not so considerate?"

"With you, my dear Anne, I have the feeling that I am with such a graceful partner that my natural clumsiness will retreat," he answered and swung me into the turn without faltering.

It was the first time in my life I had ever danced with a gentleman, the first time I had ever worn a real ballgown, the first time I had ever appeared in society, and I was breathless with the wonder and the excitement of it. I was aware that some couples had dropped out of their sets to watch and that the music was thrilling along my nerves, and then it was over, and there was a light spattering of applause as he led me back to my place next to Lady Cora.

"Anne dances like a princess," he told her. "Did you not think we made a handsome couple?"

"Very handsome," she said, but her eyes were at odds with her smile. "The next time you tell me that you have two left feet and cannot partner me, I will remind you of it!"

"It was wonderful," I said breathlessly. "Like floating on air!"

"You had best keep your feet on the ground," Lord Sinclair advised dryly. "The hounds have scented the quarry again."

Robert Glenville and Joshua Knight were indeed making their way towards me. I unfolded my fan and flapped it gently to cool my heated cheeks.

"Miss Sinclair, the supper dance is to follow directly. May I write my name on your card?" the former said.

"I shall be happy, sir." I gave him my card and continued, as he wrote his name with a flourish, "Mr. Knight, our friendship emboldens me to beg for your company during supper unless you are already engaged to take another lady in."

Yes, I know it was forward of me, but I wanted to give Robert Glenville a little set down. I do not approve of gentlemen who are too sure of themselves. And clearly he is not going to offer marriage when he learns the truth, whereas Joshua Knight might do so.

"My dear Anne," Lady Cora began in a tone of the deepest disapproval.

"I shall be delighted to take you into supper, Miss Sinclair," Mr. Knight said promptly. "I will wait for you here while the dance is progressing." He bowed slightly and moved away, having the tact not to fling any glance of triumph towards Robert Glenville.

The music had begun again. As I took my place opposite my partner, he smiled at me with raised eyebrows.

"You were grossly unfair," he remarked, "to grant me the dance and allow Mr. Knight the luxury of sitting with you during supper, when there will be more opportunity for him to talk with you."

"I prefer dancing to eating," I said softly and returned his smile as he took my hand, and we moved into the rhythm of the dance. I could see out of the corner of my eyes that my uncle had sat down next to Lady Cora and was talking to her and that Lady Cora was looking a little flustered. He had not, it seemed, asked her to stand up with him.

Robert Glenville danced well, if somewhat heavily. He was a handsome young man, I thought, but he knew he was handsome, and the wildness of his reputation frightened me a little. It might not be wise to provoke him.

"I wish the dance lasted for a longer time," he said. "You will allow me to write my name in your card for the polka?"

"I will be leaving as soon as supper is over," I said.

"You cannot!" He gave me a startled look. "One dance and then you vanish into the night? You could not be so cruel!"

"If you care to wait until after supper," I said, "you will actually see me disappear."

"Into the heavens like a star that fell to earth for a brief time?"

"Into a coach like a young lady who has not yet been formally presented," I said, smothering a giggle.

"I will call upon you," he said.

"As you wish, Mr. Glenville," I said primly, but my eyes were sparkling.

It was all great nonsense, of course, but, for the first time in my life, I was being admired and flattered, and I did not believe that I could be blamed for flirting a little.

The dance ended, and he bowed, holding my hand for longer than was necessary, not troubling to conceal his scowl when Joshua Knight offered me his arm.

"I will call upon you, Miss Sinclair," he said.

"You will be very welcome, Mr. Glenville," I said, and bobbed a curtsey before I walked away, my hand resting lightly on my companion's sleeve.

The supper rooms glittered with crystal and silver. I had little time in which to stand and admire, however, for Mr. Knight was sweeping me up to a long table laden with dainties.

"Tell me what you would like," he invited, "and I will endeavour to obtain it."

"You're very gallant, sir. I may demand something that is not upon the table," I said.

"You are far too kind-hearted to embarrass a member of the clergy," he returned, his green eyes twinkling.

"Now I will not dare to ask for anything more exotic than a little smoked salmon and some potato salad."

"And a glass of champagne?"

"Lemonade," said my uncle, coming up with Lady Cora on his arm. "My niece is not fond of wine. You have no objection to our joining you?"

"Of courst not, sir." Joshua Knight spoke with great respect, but his mobile face had fallen slightly.

"Are you enjoying yourself?" Lord Sinclair steered me to a small table, leaving Lady Cora and my supper partner together.

"It's the most wonderful evening of my life," I told him.

"You have certainly caused something of a sensation." He looked amused. "I can see that I will have a difficult task when we get to London in preventing every young blade in the city from fighting to reach your side!"

"I do not care for any of them." I lowered my voice for the others were approaching. "I liked best to dance with you."

"That's very flattering." He smiled at me briefly, but the amusement had fled from his face. "There really is no need to be kind to your old bachelor uncle."

"I was not being kind." It suddenly seemed very important that he should believe me. "I truly enjoyed dancing with you so much."

"You must never tell a gentleman that," Lady Cora chided playfully. "They are all far too pleased with themselves already! Well, my dear, one can see you are going to be quite a success. Buckfast, what do you think of your niece now?"

"What I have thought from the beginning," he answered. "She is a charming young lady who is going to be an ornament to society."

"May we drink to that, sir?" Joshua Knight raised his glass.

I was conscious of my uncle's dark eyes as they met mine, and then Lady Cora laughed and drank, and the moment was gone.

We left soon afterwards and drove back. Lady Cora alighted at her front door, waving her hand as she mounted the steps. I had expected to be full of conversation about the events of the evening, but, before we had driven for a mile, I felt myself sliding into sleep and woke with my head against Lord Sinclair's shoulder and the rosebuds crumpled in my hair.

No more now, my dear Anne,

Your loving friend, Anna.

=5=

DEAR ANNE,

I don't believe that I will ever send any of the letters that I have written, and that includes this one, but perhaps if I write everything down, I will begin to make sense of some of the feelings and thoughts that have troubled me—are still troubling me. I feel—I cannot tell how I feel since these emotions have come to fill me every waking moment. Filled my nights too, since my dreams are filled with images. I never dreamed before in all the years I spent at the Turnbull Academy.

A day or two after that ball, Robert Glenville rode up to pay his respects. I was in the garden, picking some flowers with which I intended to decorate the table for supper. He looked down at me, his eyes roving boldly over my face and figure.

"In a print dress and a gardening hat, Miss Sinclair, you look even more delectable than at the ball in roses and ruffles," he complimented.

"How very tiring it must be," I said playfully, "to have to spend time composing pretty speeches to deliver when you pay calls!"

"You are still being hard-hearted!" he cried as he

dismounted. "Does it give you pleasure to see your admirers cast into despair?"

"I am not responsible for the way other people feel."

"But you are the cause, my dear Miss Sinclair." He reached out and plucked a rose, handing it to me with a flourish.

"Your rose has thorns," I complained, as the stem pricked against my skin.

"Then it resembles your own fair self," he said.

"A necessary precaution against those who would pluck me from the bush against my will."

"Never against your will, Miss Sinclair! I came to ask you to ride with me one morning."

"I never ride save with my uncle or Adam."

"I will bring a groom to accompany us."

"And I will bring Adam," I said promptly.

Looking at me, he shook his head. "Why do I get the distinct impression that you don't trust me?" he asked sadly.

"Perhaps your reputation ran ahead of you," I said.

"How unkind of you to listen to gossip!" He was smiling but his eyes were angry. " 'Tis all the crack now to be sent down from the university—why, to actually obtain one's degree is considered vastly unfashionable."

"So is belonging to a Mohawk Society!" I flashed.

"Perhaps I would benefit from the influence of a good woman?" He put his head to one side, giving me a droll look, and, for the life of me, I could not avoid laughing.

My laughing was heard. Lord Sinclair came around the corner of the house and walked towards us.

"Good morning, Robert." His greeting was cool. "What wind blows you here?"

"Not an ill wind, sir. I came to ask Miss Sinclair to

come riding with me one morning," Robert Glenville said.

"My niece is not yet so proficient in the saddle that she can ride without leading reins. Have you been offered refreshment? If you will come in, I will have Dorcas bring you something."

"I have an engagement, sir, and merely called in as I was passing."

"Then you must not allow us to detain you." Lord Sinclair bowed politely.

"I hope to see you at the Assembly Rooms again very soon. Your servant, milord." Robert Glenville's bow was even more polite, his mouth sulky. He remounted and cantered down the drive, and I turned indignantly towards Lord Sinclair.

"I can ride perfectly well without leading reins, so why did you say that?"

"Because I do not wish you to encourage Glenville's attentions," he answered.

"Surely that is for me to decide!"

"Not while you are in my care. Glenville is not a suitable escort for a sheltered girl."

"I cannot remain sheltered all my life," I protested. "You would have me guarded by dragons, I believe."

"I would have you—"

He broke off, shielding his eyes against the sun as hoofbeats, approaching and not retreating, sounded. I stared in the same direction and recognised Joshua Knight, trim and smiling as he dismounted from a bay mare.

"Good morning—"

"Do not tell us," Lord Sinclair broke in. "You are on your way to an engagement and your route just chanced to lie through my garden."

"I am not bound anywhere save here," Joshua

Knight said. "I passed your recent visitor on the way here."

"Robert Glenville came to pay his respects," I said.

"As I do." He smiled, apparently oblivious to my uncle's brooding look.

"I would have thought," the latter said, "that clergymen had better things to do with their time than to ride around visiting."

"True, sir, but I am not yet possessed of a living," Joshua Knight said.

"And I have two to bestow." Lord Sinclair scowled.

"Which is not my reason for visiting," Joshua Knight said. "I wished to enquire if Miss Sinclair enjoyed her first foray into society and if she would come for a drive with me—"

"In an open landau with horns blowing, I suppose? My niece is not yet presented, Mr. Knight, and has not the faintest desire to be rendered conspicuous."

"Do come into the house for some refreshment," I said hastily. "I'll have Dorcas bring some coffee."

"That's very kind of you, Miss Sinclair. There is nothing," said Joshua Knight, cheerfully unabashed, "that I enjoy more than a good cup of coffee."

"I'll walk with you to the stables," Lord Sinclair said.

I left them together and went to ask Dorcas to have coffee sent in. My supposition that we would require three cups was justified. Lord Sinclair joined us in the sitting room. He and Mr. Knight were chatting pleasantly enough about local affairs, and there was nothing for me to do but pour and hand round the cups.

"And though I enjoy dancing," Mr. Knight was saying, apropos of some remark Lord Sinclair had passed, "I confess I am as happy when I listen to good music."

"In that we are of one mind." Lord Sinclair nodded towards a pianoforte at the other end of the room. "Unhappily, my own skill is minimal. My niece, however, is a consummate artist, I am told."

"Perhaps Miss Sinclair would favour us with a short piece?"

I stared at both of them, numbed with shock. As you know, I have never received a music lesson in my life.

"Play something, Anne," Lord Sinclair said.

"I—I couldn't possibly—" I began weakly.

"Of course you can. Your reports in music from the academy have been consistently excellent," he said. "Let me hear if your teacher's opinion was justified."

I could only sit, my mouth slightly open, while my mind hit upon and discarded possible excuses. Dancing had presented no problem, for I was allowed to participate in that in order to make up the numbers, but Miss Turnbull never offered me tuition on an instrument.

"I look forward to hearing it," Mr. Knight said.

"I am sadly out of practice," I heard myself say.

"All the more reason to practice now," Lord Sinclair said. "Your critics will be very gentle, I promise you."

They would be dumbfounded when they discovered that I couldn't play a note, I thought, quenching an hysterical desire to laugh as I meekly rose.

"Play something short and light. We don't wish to detain our guest beyond his liking," Lord Sinclair said, reverting to his earlier manner.

I crossed to where the pianoforte stood, opened the lid, and looked at the two rows of keys, like black and yellow teeth waiting to bite me.

"Shall I turn the sheet for you?" Joshua Knight was beginning to rise.

There was no more time to think. I closed my eyes and banged the piano lid down as hard as I could on my left hand. I felt an instant's numbing shock, and then pain ripped through my fingers, and the room shook and darkened.

"My dear Anne!" That was Lord Sinclair's voice coming from a long way off, though he seemed to be bending over me. I was half-sitting, half-lying on the couch, though I could not remember exactly how I got there. At my other side, Mr. Knight was taking a bowl of water from Dorcas. Someone plunged my throbbing fingers into the blessedly cold liquid. There was a smell of burned feathers.

"I must have fainted," I said, confused and slightly light-headed. "I never did such a thing before."

"I don't suppose you ever let a piano lid slip and fall on your fingers before either," Lord Sinclair said. "I'll despatch Adam for the doctor directly."

"No need, sir. If you will tell me the location, I will ride there myself," Mr. Knight said.

"There is no need for a doctor." I sat up straighter, more in command of myself. "My fingers are bruised, I believe, and not broken."

"We will still obtain a medical opinion," Lord Sinclair said. "Mr. Knight can call in at Doctor White's on his way back to Thornton."

"You will send to tell me if the injury is serious? I shall, in any event, return in a day or so to make my own enquiries."

"I am sure you will," Lord Sinclair said dryly. "Anne, see if you can wriggle your fingers and make a fist."

I could, though not without pain. Mr. Knight had hurried out, and Dorcas was exclaiming as she took the bowl,

"You'll require a cup of strong tea, Miss Anne."

"With a dash of brandy in it." Lord Sinclair, returning from the door through which Joshua Knight had hurried, looked down at me somewhat grimly.

"I'll fetch it at once, sir." Dorcas bustled out.

"I really do not think they are broken," I said, wincingly drying my fingers on the small towel she had left.

"If that was your purpose, you should have banged the lid down harder," Lord Sinclair said.

"It was an accident!"

"Most conveniently timed. If the idea of playing displeased you so greatly, you could have declined without proceeding to extremes—and pray do not try to lie again. You have a face that is incapable of perpetrating deception."

He was wrong. My whole existence here is based upon a deception, and, when he learns the truth, he will despise me for it. I stared at him dumbly for a moment and then burst into tears.

"Sweetheart, there's no need to distress yourself!" He sat down on the arm of the couch, drawing me to him. "If you say it was an accident, why there's an end of it! Don't cry about it."

"Shock, sir," Dorcas said, returning. "I put a good dash of brandy in the tea and poured a measure for yourself, sir."

The tea was hot and comforting, its flavour improved, in my opinion, by the brandy. I said as much to Lord Sinclair, who looked very amused.

"I hope you do not become too fond of it, my dear Anne! It would not be at all the thing to have the Honourable Miss Sinclair lacing her tea with brandy at every opportunity."

"Especially at tea parties for the clergy!"

He smiled, then became abruptly grave. "I hope that you will not encourage Mr. Knight to take the friendliness between you too seriously."

"I don't think he belongs to any secret societies," I teased.

"I am sure he is an estimable young man, though his manner is a mite frivolous for a member of the clergy! However, he comes of good family and is not without means. But any courtship must be quite out of the question."

"Am I not to be allowed any friends?" I demanded crossly.

"Friends, certainly, but I don't wish you to become entangled with any unsuitable—"

"You mean like your brother, don't you? My father?"

"Jack was wild. He had some demon of contradiction in him which made him reach out to destroy everything that was fine and decent. His strength lay in bringing out other people's weaknesses."

"And he married the girl you loved!"

I don't know why I said that. Perhaps the brandy loosened my tongue. I don't know how I knew it, but once I had uttered the words, I knew them to be true. His face darkened, closed against me. I put out my hand, but he had moved away, and Dorcas was coming back into the room with an elderly gentleman.

"Good day to you, my lord. I met the young gentleman—Mr. Knight, on my way back from a confinement—a fine boy, I am happy to say—and rode here directly. Your niece has injured her hand? Well, I am glad that you called me in. It is never wise to neglect even a sprain, for a slight injury can leave a weakness in the muscles."

I had never been more glad of an interruption. He

examined my hand, pressing and bending, and announced that I had done no more than bruise it severely.

"A cold compress and a bandage for a few days will be sufficient," he pronounced. "I don't believe there will be any need for me to call again, but if any sudden swelling should occur, I do beg you to send for me."

"We're grateful to you for coming so quickly," Lord Sinclair said. "I take it that Mrs. Richman was delivered of the boy?"

"Meg Richman, yes. Of course, the Richmans are tenants of yours! I had forgotten."

"Dorcas, you had better make up a hamper of whatever you deem necessary to celebrate the occasion," Lord Sinclair said, walking with the doctor out to the step. He did not return to the sitting room, and, a few minutes later, I heard two sets of hoofbeats diminishing down the drive.

I did not expect to see him again that day and resigned myself to a solitary dinner, but, when I came down into the dining room, having spent the intervening hours trying to rest, I found him waiting there.

"I have ordered soup and a fish soufflé for you," he said as I took my place. "That will obviate the necessity of having to use your left hand, though Doctor White informs me that after today you ought to flex the fingers gently as often as possible in order to avoid stiffness."

"I will do that," I said meekly.

We ate in silence. He seemed immersed in some darkly private thoughts of his own, and I could think of nothing to say that would repair the damage I had created.

"You had best let me pour the coffee," he said at last as the silent repast drew to a close. "And then I would advise a very early night. I am riding to York and will be absent on business for two or three days."

"I owe you an apology," I said, when we were seated in the adjoining room. He was pouring the coffee with the care of a man who is not accustomed to wait upon himself. The footman had been dismissed, and we were alone in a room that still held the last traces of sunset.

"Apologies are not necessary," he said briefly. "I do not talk very often about the past because it still has the power to cause me pain, but I realise it has become the memory of pain rather than pain itself."

"You loved my mother?"

"As passionately as only a boy of eighteen can love," he said wryly. "Lucy was seventeen, and she had a sweetness, a gentleness about her. Oh, we were both very young, but the engagement was approved. Her own parents had been killed in a carriage accident the previous year, and her only relative was a distant cousin who wished to see her settled before he emigrated to New Zealand. My own mother died after the engagement was announced, so our wedding was postponed. That was when Jack—my brother came home for the funeral."

"And fell in love with her?"

"Jack never loved a mortal soul except himself," he answered. "He was handsome, brilliant, charming, and selfish. When we were boys, I worshipped him. I was also jealous of him. I longed to be like him instead of shy and stolid. Lucy was beguiled by that dash and charm. One cannot blame a girl for preferring the spectacular to the dull, but I did blame her. I am not a man who loves lightly or forgives easily."

"And they were married," I said, very low.

"They eloped." His tone was flat and unemotional.

"They ran away together and sent back word of their wedding. It killed my father. He was a man to whom honour meant more than life itself, and he had always made excuses for my brother's wild conduct. When he fell ill, Jack did not trouble to visit him. Lucy was already with child, and Jack had a fancy to try his luck in the West Country. So, with his half of the inheritance, he built Lucy House, and with my half, I came into Yorkshire."

"You never saw them again?" I asked.

He shook his head. "We exchanged the occasional letter, but they were no more than acknowledgements of each other's existence. Lucy died in giving birth to you, and, after that, all I received were reports from time to time of Jack's drinking, of his mistresses—never visited him. Perhaps that was a fault in me. I don't know. When word came he'd been thrown from his horse during a drunken wager, I went down to Lucy House. Dorcas was coping as best she could with ramshackle guests. I believe I did have some notion of bringing you north to live with me, but you were the image of Lucy. Odd, but you have not grown up to resemble her in the least. I decided to put you in a good school and—the rest you know."

"You disliked me because I looked like my mother?"

"Illogical, is it not?" He smiled slightly. "Looking back I don't believe I actively disliked you—one cannot dislike a child. I resented the fact of your existence. When I looked at you, I was reminded that I'd been cheated of the girl I loved. It would have been unfair to both of us if I had reared you myself."

"And now?" I met his dark gaze as I put down my coffee cup.

"I am resolved to do my duty and bring you out in society," he said. "In a month or so, we will travel down to London, where you will have your formal season."

"That was not my question," I said. "I was asking about your feelings towards me now. Do you still resent my existence?"

"You cannot seriously think that I do!" he exclaimed.

"And I do not resent you," I said, "though I find it difficult to think of you as my—my uncle."

"Anne, I—" He put out his hand towards me, then drew it back before our fingers touched and, rising, went over to stare down at the leaping flames in the fireplace. "I have no family save you, so our relationship naturally creates a bond between us. I cannot pretend to be the devoted uncle, I'm afraid. We have been too long separated for that. But I am no longer the furiously disappointed boy whose sweetheart betrayed him."

"I cannot think of you as my uncle at all," I said softly. "When I compare you with Robert Glenville or Joshua Knight, they lack the power to stir me in any way."

"In London, you will meet more suitable partners," he said.

"But I will not love any of them. I will not feel—"

"I have resolved to wed Lady Cora." He broke in, his tone as harsh as if he were scolding me. "She and I have been friendly for some years now, and, were it not for my stubborn clinging to past hurts, I would probably have been married before you came. She is a smart and fashionable lady who will make an excellent wife. Do you not agree?"

"She will do everything correctly," I said dully.

"And it is time there was a mistress at Sinclair House."

"Oh, she will be very suitable." My hand was aching, and there were tears in my eyes. "She will not encourage unsuitable gentlemen to call or bang piano lids down on her fingers. She will make a wonderful hostess too."

"We have much in common."

"Which after all, is the important thing."

"Oh, Anne!" he said abruptly, looking down into the blue heart of the fire. "Why did you have to be my brother's child?"

"But I am—" I cut myself short, knowing there was no sense in saying anything, since I could say nothing that would remedy the situation. He would never forgive me for pretending to be his niece when, all the time, I am a servant of no family.

"Go to your room now. You need rest after the accident." He did not look at me, and his voice was cold. I have never seen anyone impose a more rigid command upon himself.

"We ought to talk," I began.

"To what purpose? At least you know that it was not out of personal animosity that I did not keep close contact with you during these past years. For the rest—it is a midsummer madness that will pass," he said and walked out of the room, abruptly, not glancing in my direction.

That was yesterday. I heard him ride out a few moments later, and he has not yet returned. I do not think that he will return until he has proposed to Lady Cora and been accepted. I am certain she will accept and equally certain that she will make an admirable wife for him.

Oh, Anne, when we agreed to change places for a while I contemplated only the pleasure of living like a real young lady in a fine house and enjoying a little of the luxury and the social round to which you will return. I was pleased when I met Joshua Knight, for he is the sort of gentleman who might be willing to marry me when the truth is known. But the real truth is that I don't wish to marry Joshua Knight at all!

Isn't it ironic that as long as Buckfast Sinclair believes me to be his niece, he will not allow himself to desire me, and when he discovers I am plain Anna Sayle who comes from nowhere, he will not want me at all? He will regard what we have done as the most monstrous deception, calculated to make him look a complete fool in the eyes of the world. He will not forgive me for the second betrayal of his life.

I am writing this in the bedchamber that was prepared for you, wearing a dress that ought to have been made for you. My feelings are all my own, like no feelings I have ever had before, and if you knew how heavily they weigh upon me, you would not envy me.

Your loving friend,
Anna.

III
The Gemini

=== 1 ===

THE BALL THAT would mark the Baroness Lanuit's return to social activities was occupying the attention of the entire household to the exclusion of everything else. The gowns were completed; the flowers that would decorate the hall and reception rooms being carefully nurtured by the gardeners for the moment when they would be cut; and, in the kitchen, Monsieur Louis was ordering a small army of maids as they chopped, blanched, and puréed for the sauces, salad dressings, and candied fruits that would grace the supper tables.

It was ironic, Anne reflected, as she dressed for her drive to Paris with Edouard, that she had come here to work as a servant and found herself invited to a ball. She wondered if Anna, by some twist of fate, was now dusting and sweeping. There had been no word from her, and she, herself, had sent no letters to England save the one to Miss Turnbull written by Anna to announce her safe arrival. She glanced in the long pier glass, and her lips curved in an involuntary smile. She would never be a beauty, but she was looking her best, with a sparkle in her grey-blue eyes and a fresh colour in her cheeks. She adjusted the brim of her straw bonnet and went down the stairs just in time to see her escort drive up.

"You are that rarest of creatures, Miss Anne—a

punctual young lady!" he exclaimed, descending the high step to greet her.

"I was always taught that punctuality is the politeness of kings," she said. "Did you wish to see the baroness?"

"Today I am taking a very charming young lady to see Notre Dame Cathedral," he answered. "The baroness has not requested a consultation, has she?"

"The baroness is rapidly improving in health. I believe you have worked a miracle."

"I wish all miracles were so easy. I merely gave her some sensible hints on diet and led her into a more optimistic frame of mind. If you are ready?"

"I am looking forward to it," she said demurely and felt again the ripple of excitement as he took her hand and assisted her up to the passenger seat.

They drove at a steady, trotting pace down the drive and along the highway. There was more traffic on the road this morning, and they were passed by several carriages and a couple of gentlemen on horseback.

"They are holding a market on the Left Bank this afternoon," Edouard told her.

"People go in coaches to buy their vegetables?" she asked in surprise.

"This is an antique market," he said smiling at her. "There will be some rare pieces as well as a lot of worthless stuff. I hope to buy something for my mother. Will you help me to choose it when we've visited the cathedral and eaten some dinner?"

"If you will trust me to guess what might please your mother," she returned.

"Something very French, very feminine, and of no practical use whatsoever," he answered promptly and smiled at her.

There was a warmth in him that made her feel

cherished and secure. An illusion, Anne reminded herself sternly, because their destinies lay a world apart. She would return soon to England to face her uncle's anger, and he would sail to Canada to hang out his shingle and devote the rest of his life to the care of the sick.

"A fan or a bottle of perfume?"

She pulled her thoughts back to the small problem with which he had presented her.

"I believe you have met my mother!"

"I have never even met my own," Anne said.

"Ah, yes, I had forgotten you have no family." He glanced at her. "That must have meant a lonely childhood."

"Not at all. I had the company of other children, at the orphanage, I mean. And then Miss Turnbull was always very kind."

"You sound so objective," he said, "as if you were discussing someone else's life."

"Oh, it often seems as if I am." She felt the colour rise in her face and said hastily, "The baroness has told you about the forthcoming ball?"

"She intimated that, as your friend, I would be welcome." Edouard hesitated, then said, "Would I be welcome?"

"Yes, of course. I shall—well, it is not usual to invite the sewing maid to the ball, so I will feel out of place, I'm afraid. It would help me very much if I have an escort."

"You are not in the usual run of sewing maids," Edouard said. "You are not in the usual run of young ladies at all. I cannot place you in any category."

"I grew up between two worlds, I suppose," she answered lightly. "And is it absolutely necessary to put people into categories? Cannot we be individuals?"

"I hope so." His voice was warm. "It is only that most people behave as other people expect them to behave. You do not."

"You make me sound like the countess!" she said, amused. "She is a law to herself, yet she is regarded as mad by people who will not take the trouble to see that she has rearranged her world so as to give herself the least possible pain."

"Is that what you have done?" he asked.

"Oh, I am too young at eight—at twenty-two, to have experienced much pain—and we were talking of the countess. Did you know that I have met her?"

"The lady who owns the park?"

"And the chateau beyond. She has decided to emerge from her seclusion and has invited herself to the ball, so I was sent with the official invitation."

"Was it an alarming experience?"

"More sad than alarming. Her daughter was executed during the Terror, and, from what the countess said, I gather that they were estranged. The park was opened in her daughter's memory, and the countess stopped all the clocks and lives now in the time when she felt most happy and secure."

"And she is coming to the ball?"

"Where she will probably be very shocked to find a sewing maid and a physician among the guests! The baroness insists that I attend, however, though I suspect she will not wish me to be too conspicuous. We may be reduced to dancing in a secluded corner, which is as well, for I am not a very skilful performer."

"And I," said Edouard, "never succeeded in learning how to dance a step!"

They looked at each other and laughed, and Anne thought suddenly that shared laughter had a magic about it. It was a subtle magic that blended with the blue sky and the scudding clouds, and the ribbons on her bonnet, and the little, twisting streets that wound to the heart of the city.

Notre Dame had a different enchantment, fashioned of columns of stone that rose like frozen prayers to the arching roof, of statues that seemed poised between time and eternity, of a great rose window that sang with colour. She was silent in the midst of so much beauty, conscious of the timelessness of it all and of her own relative unimportance measured against such achievement.

When they came out again, she drew a long breath of contentment.

"After that, I think a light meal is indicated." Edouard took her arm in a pleasingly masterful manner as they crossed the square.

"Thank you for not explaining things to me or drawing my attention to features of interest," Anne said.

"A cathedral like that deserves the tribute of silence," he agreed.

"Would you like onion soup, crêpes, and coffee? This restaurant makes all three superbly."

"It sounds delightful," she told him. To be eating delicately cooked food in a French restaurant with an attractive young doctor! She had never dreamed that playing the role of a maidservant would ever lead to this. . . .

"I asked you if you wanted more wine," Edouard said.

She jumped slightly when he spoke. "I beg you— no, thank you. I have half a glass still to drink."

"You were in a brown study," he said.

"I was just thinking," she said, "that when I accepted the post at Château Lanuit I never imagined that I would have such pleasant occasions to remember."

"Must they become only memories?" His eyes, so much bluer than her own, rested on her face.

"I don't follow you," she said evasively.

"At the end of the month, I sail to Canada." He spoke earnestly, holding her in his gaze. "My uncle's house is sold, and I can begin to practise medicine as I was trained to do. Come with me, Anne. Come with me as my wife."

"We have not been acquainted for long," she stammered.

"Long enough for me to know you are the wife I've been seeking, though I wasn't aware of it until we met. I know that we have only known each other a very short time, but sometimes circumstances permit us to thrust etiquette aside and act as our hearts dictate. I feel more for you than friendship. I have begun to hope that you may feel the same for me."

"You forget our positions in society," Anne began

"I am a doctor. It's a respectable profession—as respectable as that of a sewing maid."

"You have the 'de' in your name. Your family is nobly descended."

"Which means nothing in the New World, where people are judged by what they are in themselves, rather than by the name that their ancestors bore."

"I have no name at all. Anna Sayle was written on the paper pinned to me when I was found abandoned. I have no dowry."

"You have honest eyes and a fine, independent spirit. I could never hope to find another with whom I would more gladly share my life."

"Your parents—"

"Would be delighted," he broke in. "They have a

great admiration for all things that are English. They would appreciate your fine qualities of mind and spirit. Anna—for I claim the right to call you so—won't you at least consider the offer I am making? We could be wed quietly here in Paris and then travel back together. You would love Québec. There, the traditions of the Old World are blended with the vision of the New."

"You run too fast," she said. "I cannot keep pace."

"I intended to wait and then propose to you at the ball in a most romantic setting," he said wryly, "but it occurred to me that what we already share is too real and honest to be confined within an artificial situation. So I ask you in daylight, though I'll not press you for an answer until later, if you cannot decide on the instant."

She was silent, the colour bright in her cheeks. It was stupid to pretend indifference. She had been attracted to him from the first and had tried to conceal it from herself by regarding it as friendship.

"You would not be marrying a rich man," he was continuing, "but you would not be tying yourself to a pauper either. My uncle's inheritance will enable me to set up a practice and build a house. A spacious house, Anna, of rich, dark wood, with a shingled roof and a garden where you could grow herbs. I want to experiment with herbs, with their use in the prevention and cure of sickness. I believe the Indian tribes have much to teach us in that respect. You and I, together, could make expeditions into the great forests and to the lakes to seek such knowledge and bring it home again."

"It sounds wonderful," she said softly.

"It will be wonderful." His hand covered her own. "It will be better, surely, than spending the rest of your life as a maidservant, living in other people's houses, making garments for other people? I am not a man who believes that wives should be confined to the kitchen and the parlour. For me the perfect wife is also a comrade."

"But I would—" Anne bit her lip, the rest of the sentence unfurling silently in her mind. I would not be spending the rest of my life as a maid. When you return to Canada, I will return to England and make my debut in polite society.

"Don't give me a final answer now," he said. "I am aware that I have run ahead without seeking to learn the extent of your own feelings. I apologise for that, but not for the way I feel. There is nothing reprehensible about a frank and honest affection."

The two words, 'frank' and 'honest,' seared her. She drew her hand away gently from his and said, her voice shaking,

"I do beg you to believe that I am most deeply honoured by your proposal. I need time to consider it. You can understand that, I hope?"

"I hope I will always be able to understand anything you may consider is the best decision to make," he said, and smiled at her again. "But you will not blame me for hoping desperately that your final answer is in the affirmative?"

The temptation to confide in him was very strong. If he loved her, then, surely, he would find it in his heart to forgive what was, after all, no more than a harmless prank!

"I'll not press you further for an answer today," he said, "but I will ask you to remember that the difference in our stations is truly of no importance. An idle, society wife is the last partner a doctor needs. Canada would not suit such a person. Indeed, in my opinion, the heaviest burden a man can carry is a wife who has been reared to a lifetime of idle luxury."

"Shall we go to the market now and choose that gift for your mother we spoke about?" Anne said. Every word he spoke had pricked her. In a moment, she might begin to show that she was bleeding.

"It will be a tremendous help to me. I am not in the habit of picking out gifts for ladies."

He had stabled the trap in which they had driven into the city, and, as it was warm but with a pleasant breeze, they strolled through the streets towards the district of St. Honoré, where, Edouard had been informed, the market was being held.

It was hard to give herself up to the pleasures of the outing. His proposal of marriage would have to be refused, of course, but she longed to accept. To travel to the New World, to be comrade as well as wife—she dismissed the prospect with deep reluctance and tried to recapture her earlier lighthearted mood as they reached the crowded square, where booths loaded with merchandise, interspersed with larger pieces of furniture, took up much of the available space. The market was already crowded, the boothkeepers doing a brisk trade, a general air of festivity pervading the scene.

"So many items!" Anne looked round, marvelling. "It looks as if half the population was selling up and the other half buying!"

"Since the war, prices have risen sharply, and many people are delving into their attics to see what they possess that others might want to buy."

"You have learned a lot about conditions here since you came," she remarked.

"I have always been interested in people," he said simply. "When I visit a place, I like to sink into its atmosphere to absorb it and be absorbed. Then, when I leave, I carry something more important with me than souvenirs."

"Another month here and you will be the complete Parisian!"

"Another two weeks, and I will be the departing Canadian." He broke off, shaking his head ruefully. "Forgive me! I had not meant to press you further. Here are trinkets that look as if they were meant for ladies!"

"The fans are so dainty!" She took up an ivory one across which a delicate tracery of green and blue leaves had been painted. "Oh, but look! This one has a tiny mirror set in the handle, so that one may surreptitiously view an approaching partner!"

"And feign a sprained ankle if he is not pleasing? Well, I'd not blame a lady for that. My mother would find this amusing, I believe."

"There is a purse here, to match the fan! Could you not buy both for her?"

"I'll enquire the price. One bargains at such affairs, I understand. I am bourgeois enough to enjoy getting a good bargain."

"There is something a little sad after all," Anne said when he rejoined her a few minutes later with both packages wrapped, "in seeing other people's belongings sold off in the street."

"In one sense, but not all memories are happy ones. Perhaps the owners of these things wished to forget the past and begin new lives without encumbrance."

If it were possible, she thought in longing. If only it were possible!

And what, after all, was there to prevent it? The question, startling in its simplicity, blazed in her mind. The change of identities between herself and Anna had obviously been completely successful since no panic-stricken pleas for help had come from Yorkshire. Why then could the masquerade not continue? There was no need for Cinderella to flee from the palace when the clock chimed midnight. Neither she nor Anna had made close friends of any of the other pupils at the academy, and it was in the highest degree unlikely that they would see Miss Turnbull again.

If I write to Anna telling her that she can continue to be the Honourable Miss Anne Sinclair and make a brilliant marriage after all, then I can be wed as Anna Sayle and go to Québec as Edouard's wife. It would mean giving up my property, but I never cared much for wealth anyway. It will mean more to me to have a full life with the man I love—and he need never know.

"Are you weary? You're very quiet," Edouard said.

"I beg your pardon!" She turned on him a smile so dazzling that he looked startled. "Yes, I am a mite weary. Could we start back soon?"

"As soon as you wish, though for my own part any time would be too soon. But we are only ten minutes walk from the livery stables, so I can whisk you back directly."

"It has been a lovely day. I want to hold it in the palm of my hand and never let it go!"

"Does that mean that you would be willing to—?"

"Give me until the night of the ball," she begged.

"I'm sorry." He put his hand briefly over hers. "The truth is that I'm snatching at any straw. I was never in love before—never even wished to fall in love until I was at least thirty-five with my practice solidly established!"

"Until the ball. It is only a few days away," she said.

"The baroness presented me with my official invitation the last time I attended her. I did not see you."

"I was probably sewing." She gave him a glinting smile. "Sewing maids do sit down with needle and thread to earn their living, you know. They are not always sightseeing in Paris!"

"I am acquainted with one sewing maid who, I

hope, will soon be sightseeing in Québec," he answered.

"Are all doctors so persistent?" They had reached the livery stable, and she paused to look up at him enquiringly.

"This one is," he answered.

He was not a man who would take a refusal meekly, she thought. There was a dogged look in the blue eyes, and the jaw was as uncompromisingly square as her own. If we fight, she reflected, it will be clean and sharp, without ugliness or petty accusations, and, if we join hands and fight together, we will win. Already, she realised, she was coupling herself with him in her mind.

They drove back in a companionable silence. He made no further attempt to cajole her into accepting his proposal until they were turning in at the gates of the chateau, and, then he said softly, "Whatever you decide to do, I want you to know that I have been happy with you in the times we have had together. I don't promise not to try to persuade you to alter your mind if your decision is unfavourable, but I do promise to respect your reasons for taking whatever course of action you decide upon."

"I believe—" She hesitated, holding back the words until they had drawn up at the foot of the steps, and he had helped her to the ground. Then she said shyly, "I believe that you will not be disappointed in my answer, but you must not take that as a final reply."

"I will take it as the promise of one." He put one of the two packages he had been carrying into her hands. "It is perhaps not strictly correct to buy you a gift, but I saw this when I was paying for my mother's purse and fan. I hope you will consent to wear it."

"I was wrong about you," she whispered, smiling after his retreating back. "You do not fight fair at all."

There was no sign of the children, who usually ran to greet her. They were probably in the kitchen getting under Monsieur Louis's feet or with their maman in her room. The baroness still spent part of every day lying on her couch, but she no longer insisted on drawn shutters and closed windows, and the room itself smelled sweeter and fresher.

Anne went up the stairs to her own room to take off her bonnet and pelisse. In the apartment next to it, the ballgowns awaited the finishing touches. The chestnut hair and white skin of the baroness would be enhanced by the lilac and silver chiffon. Her own dress was much plainer of course, higher in the neck and with only a narrow ruffle at the hem, but it darkened her eyes to the colour of the sea on a windy day, and its simplicity was flattering to her strongly marked features. Certainly, she looked older than eighteen, but she had always been mature for her years.

"Why cannot you be as pretty as your mama used to be?" The voice, echoing harshly in the recesses of her mind, made her start violently. The image that accompanied it was equally vivid. She could almost have reached out and touched her father as he swayed before her, the reek of brandy on his breath.

For years, she had tried to remember but gained only glimpses. Now, at a moment when she was not thinking about it at all, the key had turned, and she looked down the corridors of her childhood.

Lucy House had been a handsome, sprawling house full of unexpected corners where a child might safely crouch until the current drunken rage was done. There had been fitful sunshine too—Dorcas holding her on her lap and singing a song about a pisky and papa in a good humour because there was a new lady sleeping in his bed. How could she have forgotten it all?

To avoid pain, her mind answered. Pain comes with remembering, so it's best not to remember. It's best to concentrate on learning one's lessons on facts and figures that never alter and thrust one away.

Wild Jack—that was what they had called him. There had been a darkness at his core. Baron Lanuit had a tinge of that same darkness, which was why, instinctively, she sometimes shrank from him.

If she rejected Edouard's proposal, she would be returning to England, placing herself under the guardianship of an uncle who clearly had always disliked her, holding her at several miles' length, not once writing to her during her schooldays. Wild Jack's brother, who would either resemble him so closely that she would be forced to relive her childhood again or would despise her because he had disliked his brother.

The flat package was on the table where she had placed it on entering the room. She opened it, images still whirling in her mind, and was suddenly calm and still. At the end of a gold chain, a mother-of-pearl heart was small and cool and gave promise of a future in a different place where she would never need any corner in which to hide.

= 2 =

AFTER MUCH THOUGHT, she had written to Anna, addressing the letter to Miss Anne Sinclair and marking it private.

"I have decided and hope you agree that our masquerade can become reality. We are like the Gemini stars, you and I, each as bright as the other and indistinguishable. So I will wed Doctor Edouard de Reynard and go on being Anna, and you, if you are agreeable, can be Anne to the end of the story. You will be able to make your brilliant marriage, and, of course, Lucy House and the revenues from it will be yours. And, lest in the distant future there is any question of fraud, I intend to leave a sealed letter in the hands of a lawyer here, handing my name and any moneys due to me over to you. I do not know if such procedure is strictly legal, but at least it will absolve you from blame.

"However I do not envisage any such occurrence. You are not likely to meet any of the girls who were at school with us, and if you keep away from Devon, the possibility becomes even more remote. Oh, Anna, my wish for you is that you very soon meet a man with whom you can enjoy a marriage as good as I feel mine is going to be."

One of the servants, who was going into Paris to buy some spices without which Monsieur Louis declared the supper would be a disaster, took the letter for her. Anna would certainly agree to the plans outlined in it. To be offered such a future would seem like the culmination of some splendid dream.

Meanwhile, there were the last few touches to put to the baroness's gown and a pink silk rose to sew onto Justine's sash. Both the children were wildly excited at the prospect of the ball, where they would be permitted to remain until supper time. Privately, Anne considered it unwise to allow young children to attend such an event, but this event savoured of the unusual already, so she held her peace, happy that her efforts to bring about a better state of affairs had borne such speedy fruit.

The baroness was growing daily stronger and had begun to display a real interest in the running of the household and the rearing of her children, while the baron, if he still strayed from his marriage vows, did so discreetly and at a good distance from the chateau.

The hall had already been decorated with swathes of grape ivy wreathing the white and gold columns and banks of yellow and bronze roses in the alcoves between the long windows. Beyond it, in the west wing, the dividing screens between the two largest reception rooms had been removed to create a room in which up to a score of couples could stand up, and, in the supper room, there were small tables flanking the long, central one so that the guests could arrange themselves into more intimate groups.

"Every single person has accepted," Justine said grandly. "Papa and maman are most popular, are they not?"

"Indeed they are," Anne agreed, privately thinking that curiosity had probably induced many to accept. "Stand still while I tie your sash! There! Now you look quite beautiful!"

With her dark curls bobbing on her shoulders and a smile wreathing her pale little face, Justine looked like a miniature version of the baroness.

"Do you think you can possibly contrive to sit still for the next hour until the guests arrive?" Anne asked doubtfully. "What is it, Berthe?"

The maidservant, scurrying into the room, said breathlessly, "Miss Anna, the countess is come!"

"Nonsense! it's far too early. The countess is bound to be among the late arrivals and make a grand entrance."

"I don't know about that," Berthe said, "but she's getting out of her carriage this minute, and there's nobody to receive her!"

"I'll go down at once. What on earth has possessed her to come so soon? Justine, sweetheart, go to your maman and show yourself to her."

She herself hastened down the stairs, to be greeted by the sight of the countess in towering white wig and a huge panniered skirt of purple brocade against which silver and gold embroidery glittered in competition with the jewels she wore at neck, throat, and wrists.

"Madame has perhaps mistaken the house?" Anne began tactfully, curtseying.

"Madame has done nothing of the kind," the countess said briskly. "I came to inspect the arrangements. It is so long since I was in society that I have no intention of lending my presence to a trumpery affair."

"I doubt you will find this so," Anne said.

"It all looks in pretty taste," the old lady agreed, moving towards the other wing. "The flowers are quite charming. You arranged them, I suppose?"

"The baroness supervised all the decorations."

"Ah, yes! Sophie Lanuit never did much else but arrange flowers and dabble in embroidery. Who chose the supper?"

"Monsieur Louis consulted with the baron. Would you," Anne enquired with delicate sarcasm, "care to descend to the kitchen and sample the food?"

"Sharp as one of your own pins, aren't you? The truth is I wished also to be certain that my own garments did not fade into the décor."

"Madame may rest assured that you will certainly be noticed," Anne said, suppressing a smile.

"But I will be out of fashion, eh?"

"As you must be aware, fashions now are—somewhat simpler."

"I leave simplicity to those who cannot afford anything better," the countess informed her. "Now, if there is a withdrawing room, you may escort me to it and leave me there until the other guests have begun to arrive. After that, you may have me announced."

"There is a chamber here where you will be comfortable." Anne led the way to a small parlour that overlooked the terrace. "Shall I have some light refreshments brought to you now?"

"I shall endeavour to contain my appetite until supper," the countess said dryly. "Am I to understand that you are still going to appear among the guests at this preposterous ball?"

"In a very modest capacity."

"No doubt by inviting you the baroness hopes to scotch any rumours that may be circulating about you and her husband. Nothing else could possibly explain such a—what in the world are you staring at?"

"Your necklace, Madame," Anne said stupidly.

"The pearls are rather splendid, are they not?" The countess fingered the six gleaming strands complacently. "I was able to hide most of them before I was arrested, and, fortunately, my servants are loyal and kept them against my release."

"I meant—the other necklace. The pendant. I had not noticed it until now."

"This?" The beringed hands lifted the thin chain at the end of which three small jewels were set in a triangle of gold. "I do not often wear it, but something led me to do so tonight. It is not of great value, merely a family tradition. The girls were always given these as baptismal gifts. My maiden name was De Lacy, so the jewels stand for Gabrielle de Lacy, garnet, diamond, and lapis lazuli."

"Did your daughter have such a pendant?" Anne asked.

"I followed the tradition. Antoinette du Bois—amethyst, diamond, and beryl. Why do you ask?"

"I just—it must have been very hard for you when you became estranged from her."

"She was wilful and foolish. She would never accept my advice or listen when I pointed out the error of her ways." The countess flushed with remembered anger. "I refused to recognise her marriage or to—"

"She was married?"

"Against my expressed wishes! To me she remained 'Toinette du Bois, even if she had been married a thousand times over to François Salle! And there is a name I swore never to pronounce again, since not even his friendship with Robespierre or Marat saved him or my poor daughter from the guillotine."

"If you will excuse me, Madame." Somehow or other Anne curtsied and got herself out of the room, hurrying across the vast hall and up the stairs to her own chambers. There was no doubt in her mind, even before she drew the pendant from beneath the neckline of her gown and looked at the three jewels in the triangle of gold.

'Toinette had borne a child before her execution

and, by some means, had the baby smuggled out of the prison with her baptismal pendant around the tiny neck. Perhaps she had bribed someone or her husband had had more influence than the countess allowed. And with the countess also in prison, the baby might have been hidden away in some suburb or other of Paris until passage could be found aboard ship. And then the woman to whom the baby had been entrusted had fallen sick and died.

Perhaps 'Toinette had borne the child before her arrest, since Anna had been a toddler when she was found. And, being estranged from her mother, she would have been too obstinate to inform her of the baby or to seek a reconciliation. Anna Salle—not Sayle. Anna Salle, granddaughter of the Countess du Bois and nobly descended.

"I could say nothing," Anne whispered in her mind. "Nothing need change. Anna with still have an inheritance and a fine marriage."

"In someone else's name," a relentless inner voice answered. "You will be robbing her of her own identity, of the security of knowing who she really is. Nothing you choose to give up to her can ever compensate for that."

"But that means that I will have to return to England as Anne Sinclair, to an uncle who has never taken the slightest interest in me, and will be furious when he discovers the trick that has been played upon him. And Edouard—I cannot possibly agree to marry Edouard now. When I tell him the truth about myself, he will certainly never forgive me or want me as his wife. His principles are too uncompromising."

"So you will deceive him too?" the other voice insisted. "There is the Countess du Bois also, who has become eccentric in her loneliness. You will deprive her of a grandchild she might love and cherish as much as she once cherished 'Toinette?"

There was no escaping that voice, no evading the path she knew ought to be taken. She took the pendant from her neck and put it in the top drawer of the bureau. It could stay there until the time came to return it to Anna. Meanwhile, there was the evening ahead to be endured and a proposal of marriage rejected.

She began numbly to unfasten her day dress and make ready for the ball. It would have been a great relief to be able to lie down on the bed and sob her heart out, but the guests would shortly be arriving, and it would be the height of bad manners to embarrass everybody by appearing with puffy eyelids. The emerald gown looked so charming that she was tempted to burst into tears anyway when she beheld her reflection. She drew several deep breaths, blinked rapidly to clear the haze from her eyes, and drew her fair hair back into a loose knot at the back of her head.

The mother-of-pearl pendant suited her outfit, but she could not, of course, accept it now. She wrapped it swiftly in its tissue paper again and put it back into the little box. The sooner it was returned, and the doctor dismissed, the better it would be. Amputations, she thought, ought to be swiftly performed.

"Mademoiselle, the guests are arriving." Gaston tapped on the door and put his head round it. "Are you coming down?"

"In a few moments. Go and look after Justine." She watched him run back down the corridor and sighed. At least, the children would enjoy the unaccustomed gaiety. They had responded well to the altered atmosphere in the chateau, and, for that, she could surely permit herself a little credit.

She took another look in the mirror and decided, a trifle wryly, that she looked, despite the new dress, so pale and calm that Edouard might well take her refusal in better part than she had imagined. There was about her none of the glow one might have expected to see in a girl attending her first ball.

The sounds of arrival mingled with the hum of voices and the first notes of melody from a string quartet when she reached the hall. There was a line of carriages along the drive, and the grooms were leading horses round to the stables.

There was to be no formal reception line, as the baroness still tired easily, or believed she did, if she stood for too long. She occupied one of the carved and tapestried chairs where, her lavender and silver gown artistically arranged about her, she was greeting friends and acquaintances in a charmingly languid manner. At her side, the baron, heavily handsome in his evening clothes, was the picture of a devoted husband.

"There you are!" Edouard de Reynard had detached himself from a small knot of people and had approached her.

She had hoped to see him before he saw her, to be given time to steel herself against the approaching parting. There was no time at all. He was neither the tallest nor the most striking man she had ever seen, but, with his fair hair brushed smooth and his blue eyes smiling into hers, he was the only man who mattered.

"Good evening," she said.

"I believe that it may be. One or two of the older guests remember my parents, so my stock has risen. Is it not ridioulous that my profession carries no social advantages but the 'de' in my name does?"

He was still smiling, but his eyes had flicked to the unadorned neckline of her dress, where he had clearly expected to see the pendant hanging.

She held out the wrapped parcel towards him and said in a low, rapid tone, "I do thank you for the gift but, of course, I cannot possibly accept it."

"Not accept?" He echoed her words blankly. "Forgive me, but I was already under the impression that you had accepted it."

"I have had leisure in which to reconsider," she said stiffly, "and I cannot accept it, though I am most grateful for the kind thought that prompted your action."

"Does that mean you have had leisure in which to reconsider the other matter we talked about too?" His tone was suddenly abrupt, his eyes searching.

"I have decided—not to accept," she said briefly. "I am sensible of the honour you have done me, but I cannot—"

"Cannot or will not?"

"Both," she said swiftly. "I am very sorry to have given you reason to believe that your suit might be successful but I—"

"Anna, what has happened since we last met?" he broke in. "When we were in Paris together you gave me every reason to hope, and now you are as cold as charity."

"I have reconsidered. We are not suited for marrying together."

"If it is that wretched 'de' in my name, I have told you that such considerations are of small matter in the New World."

"It is a matter of personal preference," she said tensely. "I do beg you not to press me further."

"But to refuse suddenly and give no reason! May we

not at least discuss this in a reasonable manner?" he asked.

There was complete bewilderment in his face. Anne had an almost overwhelming urge to put her arms about him and say that she had meant none of what she had just said, that she would marry him the next day and sail to Canada.

"Miss Anna, you must not conceal yourself in a corner!"

To her chagrin, she saw the baron, expansive in his good humour, coming towards them. His dark face was slightly flushed, and it was obvious that he had primed himself for this rare social event in his home by a visit to the wine cellar before the festivities began.

"My lord." Edouard bowed, his eyes still on Anne.

"You are most welcome, doctor!" The baron bowed effusively. "It is due to the efforts of yourself and Mademoiselle Anna here that the health of my wife is so vastly improved! You must save me a dance, my dear Miss Anna, for I hold you in the highest esteem." He raised her hand to his lips, kissed her fingertips and went to greet two or three more guests alighting from their carriages.

"So I have my answer," Edouard said. His voice was very low, his face white.

Anne stared at him in astonishment. For a moment she wondered what in the world could have occurred to put that expression on his face. Then he continued, each word snapped off like a thread with scissors.

"No doubt the Château Lanuit holds out more allure for you than a timber frame house in the wilds of Canada. I ought to have realized that your position here is rather more than that of sewing maid, but I am somewhat naive and colonial in such matters. Pray make my excuses to the baroness. I am called away on urgent business and will not impose myself upon you again."

He bowed and was gone, walking away from her with his head high. She must have held out the package to him as he spoke for he was carrying it.

He thought her refusal to wed him stemmed from some involvement with the baron. He believed her to be like one of the governesses with whom Lanuit had toyed and about whom all Paris had gossiped. She took a step forward, opening her mouth to call after him, then stopped dead. What did it matter what had driven him away since she had rejected him anyway? Whether he believed her to be the baron's mistress or not was of small moment since they would never meet again.

"Mademoiselle Anna, will you come and dance with me?" Gaston had come up and was bowing in a very grown-up manner.

"I am not a very good dancer, Gaston," she said.

"Neither am I, but we can dance in one of the little chambers and still hear the music."

"That would be splendid!" She laid her hand on his arm and went with him across the hall.

"Why did your friend leave?" Gaston enquired as they began to dance. The music sounded clearly from the main ballroom beyond, piercing her with its gaiety.

"He was called away suddenly."

"You have had a falling-out?" He spoke with the gravity of a child who has witnessed such fallings-out between his own parents.

"A very big falling-out." Despite her misery, she could not help smiling at his manner.

"Perhaps he will be back?"

"No, Gaston." She swallowed hard. "He will not come back."

"Then you will stay with us?"

"I don't expect to be staying for very long. There is not so much sewing left to be done."

"And you never were a governess," the little boy said. He sounded pleased.

But Edouard believed otherwise. Unwittingly, the baron had provided what looked like the reason for her refusal of his proposal.

The measure ended with a flourish. Out of the corner of her eye, she glimpsed the tall figure of the countess.

"You may have me announced now," the old lady said imperiously.

"Madame, I don't believe—" Anne found herself stammering. "The formalities have been waived."

"Obviously, since a sewing maid is among the guests! Do you expect me to sidle in unannounced as if I had not received an invitation?"

"Madame!" Gaston was suddenly a minature version of his father. "There is no need to announce you since you are the most important lady here."

"Heigh-ho!" the countess raised a jewelled lorgnette and studied him. "Chivalry is not dead in France, I am happy to find. You may escort me in, Sir Gallant."

They made an incongruous pair as they entered the ballroom, where a sudden cessation of chatter proved Gaston's opinion to have been correct. Then the music began again, and the baron, having evidently forgotten his request for a dance with Anne, went past with little Justine clinging to his hand.

"If I slip away now," Anne decided, "nobody will miss me, and I can enjoy the luxury of a long weep."

She had started back across the hall, the tears already welling in her eyes, when she heard from the ballroom a cry that silenced the music.

The countess, staring through one of the long windows that opened onto the flood-lit terrace, had uttered the cry and now repeated it.

" 'Toinette! *'Toinette?*"

Anne whirled about, but she knew already who would be standing there.

=== 3 ===

"IT IS LIKE a miracle," the Baroness Sophie repeated for the third or fourth time. "That your friend should turn up here and prove to be you, save that she is not you but the granddaughter of the countess. I know that I am expressing it all very badly, but I know exactly what I mean!"

The ball had ended, the guests having been hastily marshalled into the supper room while the countess, clutching at a bewildered and travel-weary Anna, had been guided into one of the parlours, where questions and answers had elicited some part of the solution.

"It seems," the baroness was continuing, "that Antoinette du Bois married against her mother's wishes and did not even tell her when she bore a daughter, and then the Revolution came, and the little girl was smuggled to England and brought up there as Anna Sayle, but then she and Anne Sinclair decided to change places."

"For what appears to me to have been a foolish whim," the baron said.

Anne defended herself. "It was not—or did not seem to be so at the time. I wished for a short period of independence before I went into Yorkshire, and Anna was very willing to live as a rich young lady for a month or two. We knew the deception was merely a temporary one."

"It was still reprehensible," the baron said, but his lips were twitching. "You know, from the beginning I suspected you were out of the common run of sewing maids! Well, no doubt you will not tamely settle into an idle life, or will the good doctor practice medicine in England?"

"He and I have ended our friendship," Anne said bleakly.

"So that is why he left the ball so early!" the baroness exclaimed. "You could not countenance having a mere physician as your husband, though he is of a very good family."

"With a 'de' in the name. Yes, Madame, I know."

"Well, it is your own affair, I suppose." The baroness yawned suddenly. "I declare this evening has worn me out! We will all sleep late tomorrow."

"I would like to go to the Château du Bois to talk to Anna, if I may?" Anne said.

There had been no time to receive from her friend any explanation of her sudden arrival. The countess had dominated everything with her excited questions. In the end, she had borne Anna back with her in her carriage as if she feared she might wake in the morning and find out the entire episode had been a dream.

"I doubt if you require our permission to do anything at all," the baron said. "I suppose you will be returning to England during the next few days to take up residency with your uncle?"

"He will probably be very angry," Anne said. In a curious way it was a relief to think of her uncle's anger, because it prevented her from thinking about Edouard. It was possible that he might learn the truth about her from general gossip before he sailed, but it would make no difference. He would not marry a girl whom he believed had been the baron's mistress, but neither would he marry someone who had lied to him from the start.

She went wearily up to her room, recalling how at the height of the excitement she had sped to her drawer to bring down Anna's pendant and thus give the final proof. As she took off the green dress and unpinned her hair, she reflected wryly that Cinderella had in the end her own palace to which she could return at midnight.

She did sleep late, having spent most of the night tossing and turning. Her mirror reflected heavy eyes, and her hair looked lank and dull. When she was happy, she came close to being pretty, but she doubted if she would ever succeed in looking pretty again.

Anna's sudden arrival was puzzling, since there had not been time for Anne's letter to reach her before she set out. It could only mean that Buckfast Sinclair was even more unpleasant than she had fancied. She dressed with a heavy heart and went downstairs and up the drive. She would find out from Anna the reason for her sudden arrival, and then she would make her own preparations for returning.

The gates of the Château du Bois stood open, and, as she approached the main steps, Anna came to meet her.

"Grandmère is only just risen and drinking her chocolate," she said. "We have been talking half the night! She believes that the woman who took me to England was my mother's personal maidservant and that my mother only had time to put her baptismal pendant about my neck before she was arrested. Then when we reached England, the maid fell sick. She couldn't speak English, but somehow or other she found her way to the orphanage and left me outside with what she took to be the English version of my name written on the piece of paper she pinned to me."

"Anna, why did you leave Yorkshire?" Anne broke in. "Was it so dreadful there? I have recaptured some of the memories of my childhood since I came to France, and my father was a violent, unstable man. Is my uncle the same?"

They had entered the high-pillared hall as she spoke. To her surprise, Anna took one look at her and burst into tears.

"My dear Anna!" The voice of the countess came from the antechamber. "What is upsetting you? Is Miss Sinclair being unkind."

"No, indeed, grandmère!" Anna hastened to where the old lady sat. "It is only that I am overtired and—"

"Overexcited," the countess said. "Your mother was exactly the same. Good day to you, Miss Sinclair. I have yet to thank you for restoring to me the grand-daughter I did not know even existed."

"I intended to write to Anna with word of my discovery."

"But she forestalled you by arriving! She is the image of her mother at the same age. I am hoping she is less wilful!"

"I shall endeavour to please you," Anna said and began to cry again softly.

"Nerves! I never had patience with them, but then I was never cursed with weak ones," the countess said.

"Madame, excuse me, but I do wish to know the reason for Anna's sudden arrival," Anne begged. "Was my uncle unkind to you, Anna? Is that why you are here?"

"He was very kind," Anna said dolefully, wiping her eyes. "He is not yet forty and very dominating in his manner, but not unkind. He told me that he had once been betrothed to your mother—I'm sorry, Anne, but he was! Your father stole her away, and, after she died, well, he never wished for contact with you because of the resentment he felt, but he was resolved to do his duty, and bring you—me, out in polite society. And now he is going to wed Lady Tatlock because he believes me to be his niece, and, when he finds out the truth, he will despise me!"

"Despise a Du Bois!" the countess exclaimed, jerking upright. "I should like to see anyone try! You have fallen in love with each other, I suppose! We will write and tell him who you really are."

"It's too late," Anna said. "He went to York to propose to Lady Tatlock, who has been angling after him for years. I made Adam take me to the London stage and swore him to secrecy."

"But why didn't you write to me and let me know all this?" Anne demanded.

"I did write, but I never posted any of the letters," Anna sniffed. "I kept meaning to do so, but I never did. They are in my bureau at Sinclair House."

"Where by now he will have doubtless read them." The countess snapped her fingers. "All we have to do is send to tell him you are my granddaughter and not a penniless orphan, and he will wed you."

"Because I am the granddaughter of a countess?" Anna's pretty face took on a mulish expression. "I want to be loved for myself."

"It is easy to see that she has been reared in England," the countess remarked. "The English have the most absurdly romantic notions. No gentleman of good sense is going to offer for a maidservant! One cannot expect it of him, but it seems Anna is imbued with some quixotic notion regarding the all powerful influence of love."

She broke off, staring at Anna, who was rising slowly to her feet, her eyes fixed on the window. Then she uttered a smothered little cry and rushed out to fling her arms about the tall black-haired gentleman just dismounting from a horse.

"It looks as if Lord Sinclair is not going to wed Lady Tatlock after all," Anne said.

"Then Lord Sinclair is as quixotic as she is!" The countess banged her ivory headed cane upon the ground. "Clearly, he has chased after her in the belief that she is a servant girl. I assume the baron has sent him on here for a full explanation."

"Her rank will not affect his feelings if her lack of it did not do so before," Anne said. She spoke softly, but her eyes were sad.

"Anna!" The countess rose and went to the window. "Anna, come in immediately! A Du Bois does not embrace in public!"

There was a door at the far end of the room beyond which an archway revealed a side arbour heavy with roses. Anne went through it, hurrying away from a house that had once been sad and now held too much happiness for her to perceive without the most painful envy.

There would be explanations, no doubt, and then Lord Sinclair would handsomely forgive her deception because it had, in the end, brought him happiness. Anna would become her aunt! There was a certain piquancy in the thought of the pliant Anna being legally in charge of her. No doubt she and Lord Buckfast would divide their time between England and France.

"And I will make my début and be married," she told herself without pleasure as she went rapidly along the path to the narrow gate that opened into the children's park. There were a few children still on the gaily painted roundabout, but their laughter was muted by her own sadness.

A gentleman was standing by the fountain, running his hand over the cool, green stone of the mermaid. Anne came to a sudden stop as he slowly turned to look at her and then went forward, slowly.

"I came to see the place where we had known companionship," Edouard said. "I have been telling myself that it was an illusion, but I cannot believe my own reasoning. I cannot believe that what I felt between us existed only in my own imagination. It was too real and too true. I am not wrong about that, even if at some time you and Baron Lanuit—"

"There has never been any relationship between the baron—any other gentleman and myself," she said, her voice quivering, "but I have not been honest with you. My name is Anne Sinclair, not Anna Sayle. I am in France under false pretences."

"If you have broken any law then it was a bad law!" he exclaimed. "Whatever reason you had for concealing your identity was a good reason. I am as sure of that as I am that we love each other."

"I've broken no laws." She stepped closer, her eyes searching his face. "But I have not been entirely honest about myself. How could you want a girl who is not completely honest?"

"It is honesty of feelings that are important," he said. "For the rest, no man wants a perfect wife. Perfect women lack the element of surprise that is part of their charm."

"Then I must be very charming." A smile trembled on her mouth.

"I do not know," said Edouard, "whether you are charming or not. I know only that I love you whoever you are and that I will not return to Canada and leave the meaning of my life behind me."

"It is a long story." Her hand rested now in his.

"The ship is not due to sail for many days."

"And I will likely leave bits out or tell it back to front!"

"Tell me first if you will be my wife—my imperfect, adored wife."

"I will be no other man's," she told him and was suddenly free and smiling, the memory of her father no longer too painful to bear, but touched only by a fleeting sadness.

"And the tale?" He put his arms about her. "Whatever you have to tell me will alter nothing, so how will you begin?"

"It all began," she said slowly, "when I needed time in which to write a book."

If you have enjoyed this book and would like to receive details of other Walker Regency romances, please write to:

Regency Editor
Walker and Company
720 Fifth Avenue
New York, N.Y., 10019